Annie Keary

Clemency Franklyn

A novel

Annie Keary

Clemency Franklyn
A novel

ISBN/EAN: 9783337052546

Printed in Europe, USA, Canada, Australia, Japan

Cover: Foto ©Andreas Hilbeck / pixelio.de

More available books at **www.hansebooks.com**

CLEMENCY FRANKLYN

BY

THE AUTHOR OF "JANET'S HOME"

IN TWO VOLUMES ·

VOL. I.

London:

MACMILLAN & CO

1866

CLEMENCY FRANKLYN.

CHAPTER I.

Life quivered like a rosebud in her hand,
Showing the bloom and fragrance at its heart,
Through films of beauty, not as yet withdrawn,
Waiting a warmer touch.
Queen Isabel.

THE fading light of a dull January afternoon is not usually considered favourable for the enjoyment of out-door scenery, yet it was under just that aspect of sky that Clemency Franklyn best liked to contemplate the prospect which the deep window of her aunt's drawing-room offered to her. In broad daylight, or on golden summer evenings the sights she saw thence did not tempt her to linger long within view of them. In this half-light they would better bear looking at, though even then it would not do to take any one feature of the prospect separately. The formal garden that divided Miss Arnays' house from the irregular street of the little manufacturing town in which it stood, could

never boast much freshness, and now lay blank and
leafless under a frosty sky.   The open space that
fronted it on the opposite side of the road was clearly
nothing but an unused, grass-grown coal-yard, and the
unroofed building to the right, stretching a tall meagre
column, like a threatening finger, up into the sky, was
nothing better than a manufactory in ruins.   Yet,
thanks to the dim light, its broken outlines grouped
themselves into a shape that could be thought imposing, the unfrequented ground round it kept pure
yesterday's snow—which had disappeared elsewhere—
and the broad shadow it cast over one half of the street
made the lights from the houses, and the red sparks
from the blacksmith's forge lower down, show more
brightly by contrast.   Over all, the low heavy clouds
glowed with a flickering, changing splendour—now
faint and rosy as the most delicate Aurora Borealis hues,
now deepening into a fierce red glare that faded again
before the eye was satisfied with its brightness.   It was
no natural phenomenon, Clemency knew, that thus
reddened the lowering January sky—it was only the
reflection of the furnace-fires at her father's great iron-
works five miles out of the town of Tunstall; but that
did not make the crimson light in the clouds any less
beautiful to her.   She could watch it come and go and

note the swift changes of colour without troubling herself to think of its cause. Even a less imaginative person than Clemency might have discovered a certain kind of beauty in the appearance which had pleased and awed her every winter's evening since she was old enough to peep over the window-sill.

She did not turn away from the window at last because she was tired of looking, but because she thought there were matters inside the room that claimed her attention. Most people would have considered the interior view the more inviting. Miss Arnays' pretty room was that evening arranged with extra care. Dark boughs of holly ornamented the chimney-piece, and filled two old-fashioned purple vases that occupied each a niche by the fire-place. The tea-service stood on the table, a lamp was waiting for Clemency to light it, and the whole room meanwhile was filled with the warm glow of a well built-up fire. And near the fire, sitting rather upright, in an arm-chair, was Miss Arnays, whose gentle face Clemency thought better worth looking at than anything outside the house or in. When she had taken a rapid glance round, and satisfied herself that she could not improve the disposition of anything in the room, she came forward within the circle of the fire-light, and stood for an instant considering this face. It looked a little too thoughtful, Clemency said to herself; she did not approve of the attitude in which her aunt was sitting, with her head bowed forward and her thin hands tightly clasped together as they lay in her lap. While she had been amusing herself with looking out of doors, her aunt's gaze had been turned inwards, or rather backwards, and Clemency considered it part of her business in life to prevent musings of this nature lasting too long. While she was considering by what pleasant remark she might best interrupt her aunt's reverie, a hasty knock at the door did her work for her. Miss Arnays started and looked at Clemency.

"Can they be coming so soon?"

"No, no, aunt; I know who it is. I will go to the door."

In an instant Clemency returned with a small parcel in her hand.

"I was right: it was only Arthur Yonge."

"Is he coming in?"

"No; he called to leave this parcel. Now listen, Aunt Bessie: my good genius prompted me to look into the chiffonier an hour ago, and I discovered that you had given away all our tea to Widow Betson, when she called this afternoon, and that there was positively not

a spoonful in the house. For a moment I felt wild—
then, with my usual good fortune, I spied Arthur Yonge
crossing the coal-yard to his grandfather's house. I
signed to him, and dispatched him into the town to
buy a pound of tea, and save you from the disgrace of
having asked half the ladies of Tunstall to drink tea
with you, and having nothing to give them when they
came. You are not angry with me, Aunt Bessie ?"

A slight change had come over Miss Arnays' gentle
face,—a plaintive look into her eyes, and a nervous
contraction of the mouth that never escaped her
niece's sympathising observation.

"With myself, darling, not with you. I ought not to
have forgotten to send Jane out for the tea. I wish I
had not forgotten."

"It is all right now, Aunt Bessie. Here is the tea—
and Mrs. Franklyn, clever as she is, cannot divine
through whose hands it reached us. I rather enjoy
the idea of her being indebted for her tea to Arthur
Yonge's good-nature and dispatch."

"But I am not sure that you ought to send
Arthur on messages ; he has quite plenty to do without that."

"He likes to go on messages for you, Aunt Bessie.
I should have a very poor opinion of him if he did not."

"You should have asked him to come in: it is treating him like a servant, to let him leave a parcel at the door."

"Aunt Bessie, he has infected you. You are learning to be as much on the look-out for insults to him as he is for himself. I see I shall soon be the only impartial person in the neighbourhood. I shall keep out of the feud, for 'I don't think Arthur Yonge a sufficiently important person for even Tunstall to quarrel about. However, I only failed to ask him in because I knew he would not come just now. Later in the evening, when our guests are gone, he will appear for you to thank him. He deserves some thanks certainly, for he has saved us from a dilemma. I should not have liked to have seen Mrs. Franklyn's face when the emptiness of your tea-caddy was discovered. What a story it would have been for her to tell against you in Tunstall."

"My dear, you know you ought not to call your step-mother, 'Mrs. Franklyn'; and, indeed, I don't like to hear you speak of her in such a disrespectful way."

"I know you don't; and for that reason I seldom speak of her to you. To-night you must let me say what I like: first, because it is my birthday; and

secondly, because, as I am to go home soon to the Red
House to live with her, I had better pour out all the
spiteful thoughts that are in my heart while I can. It
is the only way to get rid of them."

" I wish you would get rid of them. When I see
how little kindness there is between Rolla and you and
your step-mother, I regret that I took you both to
live with me when your mother died. I fear it is one
of the many mistakes I have made in my life. Rolla
might have had more firmness if he had been brought
up by a stronger minded person than I am; and if you
had been with Mrs. Franklyn from the first, you might
have taken your natural place as eldest daughter of
the house ; and this antagonism, this jealousy on my
account, might never have grown up."

There was a little pause. Clemency seated herself
on a stool at her aunt's feet, and taking one of her
hands she covered it with fond kisses.

" Aunt Bessie," she said at last, " please be sure of
one thing—if we are not better for living with you it is
our own fault. Poor Rolla never got into trouble while
he lived with you ; and I can't help thinking that it is
partly Mrs. Franklyn's fault that there are so many
quarrels at the Red House when he is at home. As for
myself, I might have liked Mrs. Franklyn better if she

had brought me up. If I had never known you, I might not have disliked her little stupid jealousies and petty meannesses as much as I do. I should have joined her in despising the Yonges because they are unfortunate, and in courting Mrs. Edgecombe because she is of a county family. I might even have looked down on you, dear Aunt Bessie, and seen in your goodness only an incomprehensible oddity, which one may be thankful to be without. Yes, I think that would have been the effect on me of having always lived at the Red House. I believe I am capable of being quite as vulgar and spiteful as—as other people, we will say. Acknowledge that I am at least candid, and don't sigh so deeply, Aunt Bessie."

"I was thinking how very much you had to learn, dear. It is only young people who judge so harshly. Now I can see Mrs. Franklyn's good qualities, and have a sincere regard for her. I am not surprised that she should look down upon me—so practical and energetic as she is, and I so dreamy and forgetful. Who am I, that people should not remark on my shortcomings, and laugh at my oddities?"

"You are my own and Rolla's precious real mother." cried Clemency, "and Mrs. Franklyn is not worthy to sit in the same room with you, much less to speak about your faults. But that is her knock at the door. I must make haste and light the lamp, and put the tea in the caddy before she comes in. I would not have her know the history of that tea for any consideration."

Clemency had hardly completed her tasks, when the door was thrown open, and Mrs. Franklyn and a great gust of frosty air entered the warm room together.

Miss Arnays came forward to meet her guest. It was perhaps the full lamplight falling on her face that made her look thinner, paler, more feeble than she had seemed a few minutes before; or it might have been an inward feeling of discomfort, that gave her whole person such a shrinking, extinguished appearance. There certainly was something in Mrs. Franklyn's person and manner, as she swept into the little room, half filling it with her stiff skirts and wide floating lace shawl, that justified the look of self-assertion on Clemency's face, and accounted for the nervous flush that dyed Miss Arnays' pale cheek as she held it up to receive the rapid kiss of greeting. This greeting kiss was a ceremony never omitted between the two ladies: they neither of them liked having to give and receive it very much, perhaps—yet it was far from being a Judas kiss on either side. Miss Arnays really had, as she professed, a sincere regard for her sister-in-

law, since there is a sincere regard which can consist
with a strong feeling of fear and a little personal
repugnance; while Mrs. Franklyn had such a pleasant
conviction of her own superiority to Miss Arnays, and
could look down upon her so comfortably, that she
was disposed at times to mistake these agreeable feelings for affection.

When her greetings had been made, she stood up
long enough to observe the exact position and state
of every article of furniture in the room, and to detect
the edge of the tea-paper protruding from under the
sofa where Clemency had in her haste thrust it; then
she established herself in Aunt Bessie's favourite chair,
and spread out her hands to the fire. Miss Arnays made
a feeble remark on the weather, and spoke of the kindness of her friends in venturing out on such a night to
the poor entertainment she could offer.

"Poor entertainment!" exclaimed Mrs. Franklyn.
"Well, I don't know. I am sure I always think you
seem to make yourselves uncommonly comfortable here.
Clemency must not expect such luxuries as you give
her when she comes to the Red House. This room
is far snugger than any of ours. And what a fire!
Our coals don't burn so well. How do you manage
always to get the best of everything? I suppose be-

cause you have only yourself to provide for, and nothing to care for but being comfortable."

Aunt Bessie's face fell as if she had been convicted of an unpardonable act of selfishness. "Dear me," she said, meekly, "it never occurred to me that I was depriving anyone else of these very good coals. It was Arthur Yonge who procured them for me, and I am sure, if you wish ——"

Here Clemency put a cautioning finger on Aunt Bessie's arm, but it was too late; Mrs. Franklyn interrupted with a contemptuous laugh.

"Arthur Yonge! really, dear Bessie, what a very strange person you are. Now, no one but you would have supposed it possible that Mr. Franklyn or I could put ourselves under an obligation to Arthur Yonge. Pray is he expected to join your party to-night?"

Miss Arnays turned an alarmed glance on her niece. Was there any danger of Arthur Yonge's coming in and betraying the dreadful habits of intimacy in which he was allowed?

Clemency gave her a reassuring nod, and answered boldly, "No, he will not come. He is not at all disposed to intrude on people who look down upon him."

"Then he shows better feeling than I gave him credit for," observed Mrs. Franklyn. "It would be strange indeed if he thought himself fit company for the Honourable Mrs. Edgecombe, who is sure to be here to-night, I suppose, as it is your birthday."

"But he is quite as fit company for Mrs. Edgecombe as I am," cried Clemency, hotly. "His father was a manufacturer, and mine is one. If the children of manufacturers are not to associate with country gentle-folks, I had better leave the room when Mrs. Edgecombe comes in. Aunt Bessie may entertain her : she is of the right grade—we are not !"

A flash of defiance went out of Clemency's blue eyes as she spoke ; but though she looked brave, her heart beat so quickly that she could hardly get out the words. And she wondered afterwards what it was in her step-mother's remark that had roused her to that temporary boldness. Why must she be always thrusting herself in to fight Arthur Yonge's battles ; he was abundantly capable of undertaking them himself."

An awful pause followed. Miss Arnays was truly grieved at her niece's outburst, and Mrs. Franklyn was for the moment too much disconcerted to find words in which to express her indignation. She was by no means quick at retort, and Clemency had touched the one point on which her shield of self-complacency was vulnerable. She had never discovered, during all

the years they had lived near each other, that her
husband's sister-in-law was a better educated, and more
highly gifted woman than herself. She had never even
found out that she was more self-denying, and a better
Christian; but far down in the bottom of her mind
there lurked an uneasy suspicion that some how or
other she was more of a lady; and she was consequently
subject to fits of uneasiness, lest other people should
make the same mortifying discovery.

Clemency would probably have had to reproach herself with having spoilt the peace of her aunt's evening,
if the advent of other guests had not obliged Mrs.
Franklyn to put aside her anger for a time. The little
room filled gradually, and Clemency soon had to leave
her place by the fire for fresh comers, and occupy herself at the tea-table. The entertainment was given in
honour of her birthday, and her aunt usually left the
amusement of the guests to her care. Most of them
were young girls about her own age, who had assembled
in that room every year since they were old enough to
know what a birthday was.

For many years this had been a day of days for
Clemency, long looked for and long remembered. The
girls were all her very dear friends, and yet she
had a feeling too of being something of a queen and

head among them. By general consent, she was expected to take the lead in everything they undertook.
She invented the plays, and told the stories, and originated the innocent jokes at which they were all ready
to die of laughter. Whatever might be their jealousies
of each other, they were all ready to agree that no
one was so clever, or so tall, or so pretty, or so kind as
their dear Clemency Franklyn. As years passed, and
they all emerged from childhood, however, Clemency
had found that her popularity among her companions
rather declined. She never could decide whether it
was their fault or hers that she grew more reserved,
and felt less at home with them, when they met on
each succeeding year. They had most of them been to
distant schools, while she had remained at home; and
they were now going out into a world of which she
knew nothing. When they chattered together about
their gaieties, and passed round hints and railleries
about each other's triumphs and flirtations, Clemency
listened wonderingly, not envying or despising, but
having a sense of being left out and standing alone
among her fellows. The kind of talk that she and her
aunt and Arthur Yonge usually fell into, was so different
from anything she heard from them. She had a sort of
instinct that they would think her very odd indeed if

she introduced into the discourse any one of the topics in which she was accustomed to interest herself.

Whether it was that her contest with her step-mother had ruffled her temper, or that her companions were really more exclusive than usual, she certainly found her conversational powers very much at fault on this her nineteenth birthday-evening. The young ladies would separate themselves into coteries, and all her efforts to get them to join in any common amusement were unavailing. The party who thought themselves the most aristocratic, since they belonged to the families of the principal manufacturers of the neighbourhood, and lived a few miles out of the town, were talking over the incidents of a ball at which Clemency had not been present; the town girls had their own topics, and would not have been unwilling to discuss them with Clemency, if her complacency had been equal to the task. Unfortunately, she could not bring herself to be as much interested as they were about the stranger who had sat in the Rectory-pew on Sunday; and she would not laugh at the stories of old Mr. Yonge's miserliness with which they entertained each other. They all thought it such a pity that she did not turn to better account the advantage she possessed of living opposite old Mr. Yonge's house. She might know whether or

not it was true that he went out at night to search for
stray lumps of coal, among the dock-leaves in the old
coal-yard; and she might discover whether his grandson
and his servant subsisted on broth made of old bones
and mouldy crusts, as people said they did. It was a
dreadful life for such a young man as Arthur Yonge,
who, when he was tolerably well dressed, looked quite
like a gentleman, better than most of the Tunstall
gentlemen, the girls thought, and they hinted very
broadly that they would be glad of any information
Clemency could give them on such an obscure and
interesting subject.

" Was it pride," they asked, " or shame for his
grandfather's meanness, that made him rush along the
roads with his head in the air, without so much as
looking round, whoever might be passing? They did not
think he knew one person from another in Tunstall,
and it was a pity, as right-minded people might not be
disposed to judge him harshly for his grandfather's
faults."

Some of the girls thought this display of pride and
exclusiveness interesting; others averred that they had
no patience with such airs in a young man whose father's
failure had ruined half the inhabitants of Tunstall, and
whose grandfather was a crazy miser, whom no respect-

able people ever admitted into their houses. Perhaps it was not wonderful that talk of this kind going on for half-an-hour or so should weary Clemency, but she took herself to task for feeling so much disturbed that she could not check it by a few playful words.

Ill-natured gossip about the Yonges was not worse than ill-natured gossip about others of her neighbours, who all had their turn; and she did not usually feel at a loss for words to put a stop to conversation she disliked. She was quite angry with herself for feeling tongue-tied; but she did not know that her uneasiness was so plainly written on her face, that it was discerned and commiserated by her friend, Mrs. Edgecombe, who had entered the room about half an hour before, and was enjoying a confidential chat in a corner with Miss Arnays. That keen-sighted lady watched Clemency for a minute or two as she stood silent among her companions, and then made her dejected looks an occasion for reading her aunt a little lecture on her account.

"How bored Clemency looks to-night. At her age she has no right to be bored—no, not even by Tunstall folly and vulgarity—it ought to amuse her. You are spoiling her, Bessie; having you always before her eyes she is becoming unfit for the society of ordinary mortals. I shall have to take her in hand to make her fit for every-day wear. You know I am her godmother."

"And having renounced the world for her, you are in haste to take her into it," said Miss Arnays, the beginning of a smile lightening her grave face. "No; if I give her up at all, it must be to her father and her stepmother. I have almost decided on letting her go to live at the Red House. I am too much of an invalid to be a fit guardian for a grown-up young lady."

"But I shall not sanction her going to the Red House. No; if the choice lies between her leading a hermit's life with you, or seeing the world under Mrs. Franklyn's guidance, I should say let her remain where she is. She is far above the Tunstall level; and yet you will never succeed in making her such a saint as yourself, Aunt Bessie. She is not made for a life of tranquil goodness and mystic dreams, like yours, or at least it will take a great deal to bring her to it. Look at her now, as she stands among those girls. She is like a queen among her handmaids. Look how her pretty upper-lip curls, and what a light there is in her eyes—they are liquid blue-fire. The scorn in them won't hurt anyone though, for it is half drowned in pity, there is more sweetness than contempt in her face even now. I like the way she holds her head, too—so spirited. She is full of life and thought from the crown of her head to the sole of her foot; everything about her speaks. She is quite the most beautiful girl I have ever seen. I wish I could plan her future for her. I should not be long in choosing, should I? You know what I think would be the best lot that could fall to the share of any girl. Well, I would give *that* to her, if I could."

Mrs. Edgecombe's face beamed as she spoke with as much exultation in her own generosity as if she had been bestowing a kingdom.

Miss Arnays smiled. "Don't try to get this lot for Clemency, however," she said; "don't plan it; no good ever comes of such planning."

"I am not sure of that," Mrs. Edgecombe went on; " and as for not planning, I am not a stick, or a stone, or a saint, with no will of my own, like you, Bessie. I shall go on planning good fortune for my friends, aye, and trying to have a hand in securing it for them, as long as a spark of thought remains in me. If you had an only son coming home to you after years of absence, should not you think a little about what was likely to happen to him?"

" Dear Sydney, you know I only meant to warn you against setting your heart———"

"Dear Bessie, I won't let you waste your strength on that useless warning. Have you not been warning me for twenty years against 'setting my heart,' and have I not always done it ? If I had heeded you I should have been spared plenty of pain, but my heart would have been chilled to stone by this time. Let me go on hoping to the end, even if I am always to be disappointed. My very soul springs up at the thought of happiness, and won't be crushed back again. To-night, with my son's letter in my pocket, I have a right to be happy. Bright days are coming to me at last, Bessie,—I have waited so long for them,—and I mean to take you and Clemency into their sunshine. No, I won't stay for an answer ; I have been talking to you too long. I must go and make myself agreeable to your guests, or you and I shall be in disgrace, and I had better have stayed at home this evening."

Mrs. Edgecombe rose from her corner as she spoke, and began a slow progress round the room. To most of the Tunstall ladies it was the chief point of interest in Clemency's birthday-party that the Honourable Mrs. Edgecombe was always one of the guests, and that she always came beautifully dressed, and in a sociable mood ; at other houses, no one could reckon on the state of mind she might be in, or the state of toilette. She would often

mortify the most obsequious hostesses by refusing to
shine when they most wanted her to do them honour.
Miss Arnays would have been satisfied to have her
friend in any dress, and in almost any mood; but Mrs.
Edgecombe chose to be worldly wise on her behalf.
For that one evening she valued the consideration her
rank and position in the county gave her, because she
felt it enabled her to raise her meek friend in the
opinion of the neighbours, who had not eyes to discover
her real superiority. She enjoyed snubbing Mrs.
Franklyn, and deferring to Miss Arnays before them
all; it gratified her love of rule and her generosity at
the same time. Her tactics were quite thrown away on
Miss Arnays. Clemency comprehended them, but could
not make up her mind whether she approved or not.
Her reverence for her aunt lay deeper than Mrs. Edgecombe's, and she had rather have had her undervalued
than made much of for other than the right reasons.
What she did quite appreciate, however, was the tact with
which her friend brought the discordant elements of the
company into harmony, and introduced among them
good humour and a disposition to be amused. Five
minutes after she had joined the group among whom
Clemency had stood so silent, there was plenty of
rational talk, and soon frequent bursts of genuinely

happy laughter. One or two rather forward young
ladies received a check when they attempted to pre-
sume too far on Mrs. Edgecombe's favour, but it was
not conveyed in words ; a slight look of surprise on her
face, a slight elevation of the eyebrows, was enough to
convey the lesson required, and then they were allowed
to bask again in the bright smiles, and to be won by
the gracious ways that had charmed more critical
assemblies than this Tunstall one. Clemency found
herself taking an eager share in what was going on, and
forgetting to listen for the striking of the clock, or to
wonder how other people were getting through the
evening. The only person who held aloof was Mrs.
Franklyn, and her silence was for once no symptom of
displeasure. She was wholly absorbed in an anxious
study of the various items of Mrs. Edgecombe's dress,
under the delusive idea, that if she could reproduce it
exactly, her own square person and florid face might be
made to look as graceful and winning and young as
those of her model.

Mrs. Edgecombe was in reality some years the elder
of the two, and her face had long since lost every trace
of bloom ; the look of youth, which everyone attributed to her, belonged to her mind more than to her
body. So much youthful enthusiasm and hopefulness

as still shone through her eyes and lighted up her changeful face, Mrs. Franklyn had never known at any period of her life.

Later in the evening, when the fathers and brothers of the young ladies had called to escort them home, and when there was no danger of the conversation flagging, Mrs. Edgecombe drew Clemency into a corner to indemnify herself for her exertions by having some quiet conversation with her favourite.

" I want you to congratulate me," she said, suddenly taking the young girl's two hands in hers and pressing them warmly. " I have heard some very good news to-day, and no one has said yet that they rejoice heartily with me. You shall guess my news."

" It is something about your son," said Clemency, smiling; "you would not be so happy about anything that did not concern him. He has distinguished himself further ; or some fresh honour has been paid him."

" Better than that. He has distinguished himself so often already that even I am satisfied ; besides, you know, the war is over. My news is, that in one month he will be at home, to remain with me certainly for two years ; perhaps always."

" What, will he leave India ? I thought you told me last month that some very important appointment had been offered to him, and that he was very happy about it."

"Yes; and I was in despair. I thought I was being punished for having made him ambitious, for that ambition was dividing him from me. I did not know then how very good he is. He got a letter from me complaining of my loneliness and my longing for him, and he immediately threw up his appointment, though it was the reward for his distinguished conduct during the war, and must certainly have led to higher honours. Devoted as he is to his profession, he gave up all to come to me."

"And you are glad."

"I am his mother, Clemency. I would not have asked him to do it for the world. I never meant him to interpret my letter as he did; but since he has made this sacrifice of his ambition to me, I must rejoice in the prospect of having him safe at home. It will be so different from any other time when I have had him. I shall be able to do more for him than I have ever done. He left Combe eight years ago, because even I could not then make it a happy home for him. Now he returns to be its master. Ah! God forgive me if I am too glad."

Mrs. Edgecombe drew one of her hands from Clemency's and shaded her face, over which a quiver of pain was passing. Clemency looked away, sympathising with this sudden revulsion of feeling. She remembered that it had been the late Mr. Edgecombe's tyrannical disposition and violent temper that had driven his only son from home, and she respected the scruple which made his widow half afraid of indulging her joy at this son's return lest a sense of relief in her husband's death should mingle with her happiness. This momentary interruption checked the flow of confidence; before Mrs. Edgecombe was ready to talk again, some of the guests had risen to take leave, and Clemency's attention was claimed in other parts of the room.

Tunstall kept early hours. By ten o'clock Miss Arnays and Clemency had once more the drawing-room to themselves; but the gossips of the place would have been scandalised if they had known that even then, late as it was, Clemency had not received all the congratulations she was destined to have on her birthday. Just as she and her aunt were preparing to wish each other good-night, the drawing-room door opened again, and the tall figure of Arthur Yonge presented itself in the doorway.

"I am not coming in," he said, in answer to an invitation from Miss Arnays. "I know it is too late for me

to come in; but I have something here which I want
one of you to come and take; it is worth crossing the
room for."

"Ferns and Christmas roses. Oh, how beautiful!"
cried Clemency. "So you have not given up the
fernery after all. I thought you said you must?"

"I must : my grandfather won't keep the room warm
enough for the plants to come to any good. For his
own sake, I tried to persuade him to do so—he needs
warmth as much as the ferns; but it almost broke his
heart : so I thought it best to give up the struggle. I
determined to keep my poor ferns alive till after your
birthday though, and now I have gathered all the
fronds—here they are."

There was a slight sadness in the tone in which these
words were spoken that did not escape Miss Arnays'
ear.

"Come in, and give them us yourself, Arthur," she
said, kindly.

"But my feet are wet, very wet."

"Then pray come in ; come to the fire."

The first step over the threshold taken, he crossed
the room and settled himself in a low chair by the fire
with the air of one quite at home there.

It was a pleasant, honest, strong face on which the

light of the fire fell, well-featured enough to be thought handsome by casual observers even, and so full of expression that those who knew it intimately took little note of any other perfection it might fairly claim.

"I wish it were not so late," he began, casting a wistful look all round the pleasant room. "I wish my conscience would let me stay with you. What a long evening it has seemed. I thought that last set of people never would go."

"You were not walking up and down the street, spying upon us, were you?" exclaimed Clemency. .

"Only for the last hour. My grandfather always rakes out the fire and goes to bed at nine. I generally read in my room; but to-night I could not settle to anything."

"How cold you must have been," said Miss Arnays, compassionately. "I am glad you came in here to the fire."

"I hope though you don't think I came here to escape the cold?"

"Why not?" cried Clemency; "do you want us to think you too sublime to feel cold?"

"If I believed you really thought I came here for the sake of the fire, I would not enter the house again till April."

"What a terrible threat! Really, Mr. Yonge, you ought not to come in so late at night and disturb our minds by holding such a calamity as that over our heads."

"I wish you would speak seriously," said Arthur.

"Why must I? I have been weighing my words all the evening. May I not feel at liberty to say what I like now?"

Clemency's blue eyes danced and sparkled as she spoke with a gaiety that had been wanting in them all the evening. Arthur Yonge's face showed a determination not to be mollified too easily.

"I don't believe you have been weighing your words," he said. "I believe you have been laughing, and talking, and enjoying yourself among all those people thoroughly."

"Well, have I not a right to enjoy my birthday? How could I tell that you were walking up and down sulkily in the cold all the time? You might have come in if you had liked."

"No, thank you: I prefer the cold and the outside of the house to this room with all the gossips of Tunstall in it."

"What is the matter with you to-night, Arthur?" said Miss Arnays. "I don't understand what you and Clemency are quarrelling about."

"He is in a contradictory humour, Aunt Bessie. Turn him out into the cold, which he says he likes so much, for he is resolved to be disagreeable."

"I believe I am feeling very cross to-night, and that I had better go. The truth is I can't bear to have my idea of your room spoiled even for a single evening, Aunt Bessie. When I am sitting at my work in my room opposite, I like to look across and see the lights streaming from your windows. I don't feel much tempted to grumble that I am not with you; but it is quite another thing when other people are here and I away."

"You are very ungrateful to the other people," said Clemency, slyly. "If you had only heard how some of them concerned themselves about you!"

"Good-night; I am going," interrupted Arthur. "I won't stay to be made crosser still. Won't you take the ferns? They look better already for the warmth of the fire; but the Christmas roses are drooping."

Clemency took the bunch, which filled both her hands, and buried her face for a moment among the green leaves, while she inhaled the faint perfume of the flowers.

"I do like Christmas roses," she said, looking up.

"I don't know how it is, but their faint scent makes me think of all the summer-flowers that are coming after them. It seems to promise all sorts of sweet and good things for the year. I am glad to have a bunch on my birthday. Thank you for bringing it."

Arthur, who had now risen from his chair, came a step nearer to her. "I had nothing else to bring, except, if there had been time, I meant to have told you a piece of good news to-night. It only concerns myself, but if I had had time I meant to have told it you to-night."

"Tell us : Aunt Bessie and I always like to hear good news. It is curious that two people should have told me good news on my birthday."

"Two people! Who else has told you anything?"

"Mrs. Edgecombe : her son, Major Edgecombe, is coming home from India in a few weeks to live at Combe."

"Oh! well I suppose my news will sound very tame after that. It is only about the success of my experiments on the ironstone, from that mine at Vale Combe which used to belong to my grandfather, and which is never worked now. I explained all about it to you once."

"Yes, I remember : the stone is of no use, because there is too much something or another mixed with it."

"Yes; and I think I have discovered an easy method of getting this something—phosphorus it is— out. I am not quite sure. I can experiment only on so small a scale—want of fuel and want of money hamper me so. Yet I think I have hit on the discovery my father was always trying for. It is as simple as Columbus's egg when one knows."

" Will it be very important to you ? " asked Miss Arnays.

" I dare say not. I shall never be able to make any one believe me or attend to the common sense of the thing. Not in Tunstall, at least, where they all creep on in the same old groove, and where my father's reputation of being a theorist has descended to me. It would require a great deal of money to work my discovery so as to turn it to good account. However, I am glad it is made. It proves that my father's views were right in the main ; that he was reasonable in his expectations, and did not sacrifice other people's interests to an utterly unfounded hope. Some day, years hence, I may make the good folks of Tunstall acknowledge this."

"You will?" cried Clemency. "Oh, I call this excellent news ! I wonder you can tell it so quietly. It is what we have so often planned. Why don't you look pleased, Aunt Bessie ?"

"You see even Aunt Bessie does not believe in me," said Arthur. "What must I expect from other people?"

Aunt Bessie smiled a little sadly.

"My dears, it is one of the penalties of being old, and having seen many disappointments, that one cannot believe in good news as heartily as one could wish. There—I wish you had not been so quick to read my face. I did not wish to damp anyone's spirits, and this is the second time I have done so to-night."

CHAPTER II.

In quella parte del libro della mia memoria, dinanzi alla quale poco
si potrebbe leggere, si trova una rubrica la qual dice : *Incipit Vita
Nova.—Dante.*

THE high street of Tunstall was still busy with
comers and goers, and the windows of the shops and
houses were alive with the reflection of the lights
within, when Arthur Yonge left Miss Arnays' house, but
as soon as he had crossed the road and turned down the
lane into which his grandfather's garden gate opened,
he found the stillness and darkness of midnight. There
were no lamps along the lane, and no glimmer of fire
or candle from either of the two large buildings that
opened into it. Only from the reflected red glare
which Tunstall was never without on its darkest nights,
had he light enough to distinguish the dilapidated garden gate, overhung by two forlorn weeping willows, and
when with some difficulty he had made it turn on its
crazy hinge, and let him in, he was able to walk down
the worn, weedy gravel walk, quickly and safely, only
because he knew every one of its ruts and pitfalls by

heart. Twenty years before, this great garden of Mr.
Yonge's had been the pride of Tunstall. It was not
then considered a defect, that it was only divided by a
high brick wall from the coal-yard and outworks of Mr.
Yonge's iron foundry. In those days most of the Tunstall manufacturers liked to live within sight and
hearing of their places of business; and neither old
Mr. Yonge nor his son, Arthur's father, had ever
dreamed of feeling anything but satisfaction in the
neighbourhood of theirs. The smooth grass plat, and
broad gravelled walk, flanked by its rich fruit wall,
would not have seemed pleasant places for them to
walk up and down in the evening, if the sound of
the forge hammers had not reached them there. When
Arthur was born, the garden, so still to-night, had
never known a moment's silence, night or day, for
many a year; but to those who could bear noise it had
been a pleasant and even a pretty spot. Arthur's
mother had had a great taste for flowers, and her
husband had indulged it by filling the grounds with
every variety of plant or shrub that would flourish
in spite of the coal dust. All trace of careful cultivation had vanished now, as completely as the clang of
hammers and hum of business had passed away from
the forges and yards beyond the garden. A stagnation

as of death had fallen on all. The entire premises, once the most frequented spot in Tunstall, might as well have been blotted out of existence for any use they were to the inhabitants of the place now, or for any heed that was taken of them. Strangers passing through the town were wont to point out the ruined manufactory and neglected house, and to ask if their disuse were not a proof that the trade of the place was declining; and the question, if put to a zealous upholder of Tunstall, was sure to bring out a longer story of old Mr. Yonge's past career and misfortunes than an indifferent person cared to hear.

Once this history of Mr. Yonge's failure had been the absorbing topic in Tunstall, and there were very few who could speak his name without indignation or pity. So many people had suffered through his change of circumstances, so many had been indebted to him for kindnesses in the time of his prosperity, that it took a great many years of hermit-like seclusion on his part to make his existence, so nearly forgotten by his neigh bours, as it now was. For fifteen years he had never been outside his garden gate in the daytime; never exchanged a word with any one who had known him in former days, and yet there still were a few people who occasionally discussed the question which had once divided the town, whether he were to blame or not for the catastrophe which had sunk many other fortunes as well as his own. These people said that if his former partner, Mr. Franklyn, had not chosen to desert him, just at the moment when he did, or if his son had lived a little longer, or even if the old man's mind had not given way so inopportunely, affairs would have assumed a different aspect, and the trade of Tunstall might have been spared the severest shock it had ever sustained.

It was, however, idle to discuss such possibilities now. Whether by fair means or false, Mr. Franklyn had long ago succeeded in making himself the most important personage of the neighbourhood; and Mr. Yonge only influenced the fortunes of the town by the strange obstinacy which induced him to keep the old house and its extensive premises in his own hands instead of letting them and living comfortably elsewhere on the rental, as he had been urged to do as long as he had friends who cared to press advice upon him.

No one had a right to prevent his indulging this whim, for the house had been settled on his son's wife, and the creditors had no claim on it; and though year by year, as it fell into drearier decay, it became a less suitable abode, there were also year by year fewer people who concerned themselves with the wisdom or folly of the obstinate old man's doings. Arthur had dim, but very dim recollections of his home under a very different aspect from that it wore now. He could remember, but it seemed to him like a picture from another life than his own, that he had one day sat upon the landing of the wide staircase and watched the arrival of a riding party at the front door; he recollected seeing through the open door the horses led away; and then the entrance of a tall, fair-haired young man and a lady in a riding-habit into the hall. He remembered that he ran downstairs to meet them, and that the young man lifted him on his shoulder, and that the lady looked frightened and begged him to take care. He always thought it was the pretty look of tender anxiety on the lady's face that had impressed the little scene on his childish memory.

One other remembrance, and only one, rewarded his anxious efforts to recall those early days. He had a picture in his mind of a well-furnished nursery, cosy and warm, with the glare of a dying fire and of a rushlight in it, and of himself sitting up in bed crying at some childish fright or pain. Then he remembered two faces appearing, one on each side of the bed, a man's and a woman's, and bending over towards him: the features of those faces were dim; he could not force his memory to give them back, but he could recall soft words, and such caresses as had been foreign indeed to any other part of his life. The next thing he recollected clearly was being lifted up to a window to see a long procession of black carriages pass slowly down the gravel walk. He knew this must have been his mother's funeral, for his father's, which occurred three months later, had been marked by no such outward show of mourning. There must have been a long blank in his memory after that, for it seemed to him that the old house became all at once such as he ever afterwards knew it. He had no recollection of any great change or terrible loss. His life seemed to have glided naturally into the stillness and solitude which made his childhood so very different from that of the other young people he afterwards knew. It was not an unhappy time. The empty rooms were splendid play places, and he was too full of life and energy to mind much having them all to himself. From his grandfather and the old female servant, who were the only other occupants of the house, he had much neglect, but never any unkindness. Sometimes, when he had discovered some very great treasure, a variegated snailshell in the garden, or a very available piece of broken board, or fragment of torn damask in one of the dismantled rooms, he would seek out one or other of them and try to make them sharers in his satisfaction. Neither the old man nor the old woman ever repulsed him on these occasions; they listened, the one dreamily, the other stupidly; but as Arthur never had any other auditors, he was satisfied with the amount of sympathy they gave. Sometimes he would require them to take a part in one of the dramas, "fragments from his dream of human life," which he was always acting; they obeyed him passively; they allowed him to lead them from room to room; they stood, and spoke, and looked as he desired them to do; and the vividness with which he realized his own conceptions made up for the want of understanding and interest with which they played their parts.

It was a curious relationship which existed between the child and his two aged guardians; there was too little sympathy between them to make it a living tie. Standing on the opposite shores of life, they had so far to look across that their vision of each other was very indistinct and dim. They tolerated each other; but there were scarcely any points on which their lives touched. Arthur's nature was able to develop and take colour in this sunless moral atmosphere, partly because of his natural healthfulness and vigour, partly because he did not depend wholly for mental culture on his human companions. He had learned to read very early from his mother, and a small store of books which she had brought into the house with her had been rescued from the general wreck, and stored away in a closet in one of the rooms to which he had access. Some were well-thumbed volumes which had delighted her childhood, some were her girlish school prizes, some had been gifts on her marriage.

Arthur was about six years old when the contents of this closet began to have attractions for him. He had lost the habit of reading, and at first he contented himself by turning over the leaves in search of pictures. The pictures, however, aroused his curiosity ; he was driven to seek information in the text of the book, and, as he had a great deal of perseverance and a strong will, he never rested till he had made out what he wanted to know. When he had taught himself to read with ease, the closet offered him endless store of happiness. He used to spend whole days seated on the bare floor of the room that had been his mother's boudoir with a book on his knees. Reading thus without any older head to guide his studies, the ideas he gathered were often grotesque and incorrect, but never failed to be vivid. If there was no one to explain, there was also no one to put in the disenchanting words, " It is not true," " It is all a fable," by which grown-up

people destroy a child's delightful visions. Everything
he read was to him equally true and real, and his conception of the world beyond his own town was large and
varied enough to admit every realm of fairy and home
of legend with which his mother's library made him
acquainted. The Peacock Kingdom, and the country
where the nose-trees grow were quite as grave localities
to him as the little wicket-gate and the interpreter's
house, and the land of Beulah. Being naturally of a
reasoning turn of mind, he exercised his powers by
trying to reconcile the various accounts of the world
he came across. He puzzled himself endlessly to discover how it was, that the Prince who went to purchase
dogs for his father did not come across Mr. Legality or
fall into the Slough of Despond, and why Christian did
not one time or another wander into the White Cat's
dominions. Unnoticed by any one his judgment
strengthened and his mind grew, while his thoughts
were thus strangely occupied.

When he was ten years old, a school friend of his
father's passed through Tunstall, and called on his
grandfather. The interest with which the neglected
child inspired this gentleman induced him to make
some representations to old Mr. Yonge, which ended
in Arthur's being sent as a day scholar to the Tunstall

Grammar School. This event did not all at once produce such a change in Arthur's life and habits of thought as might have been expected. His schoolfellows were not disposed to be sociable with him, for old Mr. Yonge's reputation for oddity and miserliness caused them to look upon him with a certain distrust ; and Arthur had lived so long alone, that he had not the manners or accomplishments that would have won their good will. He came and went always alone to the schoolhouse ; he learned his lessons, or dreamed over his books, on the school forms; and followed his own thoughts among the crowd of young faces in the play-ground almost as uninterruptedly as he had done in the solitary garden.

The event which changed him, by waking the first spark of real affection and human interest in his heart, came upon him a year later. It was a very trifling circumstance, but it began a new era of existence for him. He was returning home rather later than usual one summer's afternoon, having been kept at school to learn a neglected lesson, when on turning down the lane he saw a crowd of schoolboys assembled round the gate of his grandfather's garden ; in the midst of them stood a little girl who appeared to be talking to them eagerly, her bonnet had fallen to the ground, her small face was flushed, and her blue

eyes were flashing with indignation. All this Arthur
observed as soon as he entered the lane. When he
reached the gate, he discovered the cause of the com-
motion. His schoolmates had been hunting a cat
down the road, and it had taken refuge in the willow-
tree that hung over Mr. Yonge's garden wall. The boys
were discussing how best to dislodge their victim, and
the girl, having planted her back against the gate to bar
their entrance into the garden, was pleading its cause
with all the eloquence in her power. Her words were
little heeded, however, and two of the bigger boys were
hoisting a smaller one on to the wall when Arthur
came up. He knew his own wall better than they did ;
he gained the top first, sprang into the tree and caught
the panting creature in his arms ; then he swung himself into the garden, ran a few paces, and set it free
among the tangled high grass of the lawn. The schoolboys raised a shout of anger and disappointment at
this sight, for they were too much in awe of Mr. Yonge
to pursue their hunt into his premises.

Arthur ran back to the gate. "It is safe," he said to the
little girl, who was now looking anxiously through the bars.

"Oh, I am so glad !" But as she spoke her blue
eyes, that had been flashing so indignantly, filled with
tears, her little lips trembled, and a sound between a

gasp and a sob came from them; for now that the excitement was over, her courage began to give way. Arthur looked at her, half with dismay, half with a new sense of fellowship and power of protection.

"Don't be afraid," he said, stoutly. "No one shall hurt it now. I won't let them."

The child raised her face to him; both trouble and anger went out of her eyes, and instead there came a look of confidence, the remembrance of which never afterwards passed out of Arthur's memory.

"I know you won't," she said. "You are a good boy: I like you."

Just then a tall gentle-looking lady turned down the lane; the rude schoolboys retreated as she approached, and the child picked up her bonnet and began to arrange ·· on her head.

Arthur heard the lady call the child Clemency, and express some surprise that she should have run so far away from her, and then they turned and entered the garden of a house on the opposite side of the way. All that evening and many days after the child's words rang in Arthur's ears, and made a song in his heart— "You are a good boy: I like you"—his thoughts and dreams began to take a colour from them. He wondered less about the stories he read, and lived in them more. When he read of any wonderful adventure or generous deed, his heart beat quicker than it used to do; for the possibility that he too might do brave actions occurred to him, and then he thought the little girl, with the wonderful blue eyes, would say again, " You are good : I like you."

About a week after his adventure he met Clemency and her aunt in the lane again, and they stopped and spoke to him. The grave face and soft voice of the elder lady awed him at first, but when she had spoken to him once or twice he began to look forward to these chance meetings as to the great events of his days. One Sunday afternoon Miss Arnays, seeing him idling about the lane, invited him into her house, and during the evening she made such discoveries respecting his ignorance on the subjects she considered most essential, as filled her kind heart with pity. From that time it became an established custom that Arthur should spend every Sunday afternoon and as many of the holiday hours of his week days as he chose at Miss Arnays' house. It was his real home, yet it never grew so familiar as to lose the halo of glory and happiness with which he had invested it when he had pictured it to himself as the abode of his little heroine. He and Clemency learned their lessons together, and shared each other's childish scrapes, and had their little quarrels and jealousies; but even while tyrannising over her, and bringing her into very perfect obedience to his will in all practical matters, Arthur continued to refer to her in his thoughts as a sort of outside conscience. Her expressed approval remained his ultimate reward for all present exertions, and for all fancied triumphs in the future. Miss Arnays ruled them both by the power of her perfect gentleness. If she had been less just or tender; if there had been any tinge of self-seeking or self-love in her character, she might have found the task of ruling two such eager impulsive natures beyond her strength. As it was, the weakness of her will only enlisted their generosity on the side of obedience. They knew she was always right, and they —Arthur especially — felt a pride in yielding to her gently-expressed wishes a submission she would not have known how to exact.

Time passed on. Clemency grew tall and fair ; her step-mother reminded her often that she was no longer a child. Her aunt observed gladly, that in spite of the alteration years had made in her outward appearance, she remained a child at heart, as simple, as fearless, as happily occupied with outward things, as unconscious of herself, as she had been at ten years old.

Arthur, on the other hand, passed rather suddenly from a happy, confident youth, into an anxious manhood. His circumstances remained the same, but his understanding of them altered. As greater knowledge of the world came, the limits which hedged in his future prospects, and baulked all the ambitious schemes he had ever formed, grew clear to him. When he had gained the head of the Tunstall school, and learned all the masters there could teach him, he found himself thrown on his own resources to determine his next step in life. His class fellows drifted off to college, or were sent elsewhere to study for the professions they had chosen; while he who felt he had it in him to surpass them all, had no such help offered to him. Sometimes he thought of writing to the friend who had placed him at school, and asking him to supply the means for finishing his education away from Tunstall; but apart from his dislike to ask so great a favour from one on whom he had no claim, there was a consideration that always obliged him to put the wish aside, when he had entertained it a little while. His grandfather was growing feebler in mind and body every year, and more strongly possessed by his mania for saving. Of late Arthur had assumed a gentle control over him, and it was only his influence, or rather authority, which pre-

vented the old man from inflicting the most terrible
privations on himself. After much thought, Arthur
came to the conclusion that he could not leave his
grandfather to fall a victim to his own sordid fancies,
though the prospect of spending the best years of his
own life in defending him from them was dreary enough.
Often, very often, a longing for change, for escape from
the petty contentions which every day brought with it,
came strong upon him; but having once made up his
mind that it was his duty to stay, he stayed, and no
one, not even Miss Arnays, ever heard him complain of
his lot. There was an alteration in the expression of
his face, which told of a past struggle to those who
cared to read it; his eyes lost something of their old
confident light; his lips closed in a graver, firmer line,
but that was all.

He did not remain idle because he could not follow
the profession he would have chosen. He succeeded in
obtaining employment as clerk in the manufactory of
a gentleman with whose son he had been at school, and
his active mind soon led him to feel a greater interest
in the work he saw going on round him than he had
believed possible. His father had been a skilful
chemist, and had spent much time and money in
endeavouring to discover fresh and more perfect

methods of preparing the mineral stone which the mines round Tunstall yielded. Some of his experiments had been tried on a very large scale, but up to the time of his death he had not attained any satisfactory result. The notes he had made of his unsuccessful attempts, and many of his books and implements, came into Arthur's possession. He had only valued them as relics of his father, till his interest in the subject of which they treated had been roused by the nature of his daily work. Then he turned to them with new understanding and curiosity, and soon found the study so absorbing that he devoted to it every hour he could command. The ambition which he thought he had resigned awoke again ; and as he followed the course of his father's researches, and understood how near success he had often been, he set before himself as an object, to complete the work to which his father had sacrificed life and fortune. His hopes of success were at times very high, and then again low ; and he always knew, even when he indulged in the brightest visions, that the discovery, when made, would not be of the same use to him that it would have been to his father. He generally told himself that it was more for his own satisfaction than with any prospect of achieving fame or fortune that he pursued his labour with so much zeal.

Miss Arnays and Clemency were the only confidants he had of his schemes and hopes. The happiest hours of his life were still those which he spent in their company; while these continued happy, he thought he could well bear any trouble that fell upon the others; but in proportion as he valued his intercourse with his only friends, he grew jealous of any interference that came to spoil his pleasure in it. Miss Arnays often scolded him for being so exacting; and during the last few months he had sometimes been himself surprised at the vehemence of his discontent when some chance visit from Mrs. Edgecombe, or Mrs. Franklyn, had banished him from her house during the hours he reckoned on as his own. To-night, as he groped his way down the dark garden, his thoughts were full of the piece of news Clemency had told him, and he reflected on it with anything but satisfaction. The idea of a new intimate being introduced into their circle did not please him at all. Arthur foresaw plainly that there would be many lonely evenings during the coming summer, which would be quite spoiled to him by the absence of his friends, or visits to Combe, or by the presence of Mrs. Edgecombe and her son in his place in Aunt Bessie's little drawing-room. Why could not Colonel Edgecombe have stayed in

India? Before Arthur reached the house he had conceived a strong dislike to this individual, and conjured up a picture of him which it consoled him to contemplate. He was sure to be just such another pompous, irritable, weak, obstinate fool as his father had been. If Arthur could only have felt equally certain that other people would be as ready as he was to see Colonel Edgecombe in a just light, and as little disposed to invest him with heroic qualities suggested by his circumstances, he would have borne the prospect of his return with indifference.

As it was, enough irritation remained to make him more than usually sensible of the dreary appearance of the wide empty hall into which he let himself. The sounds he made in shutting and locking the front door woke a hundred busy echoes in the deserted rooms, and the rush of wintry wind which had entered the house with him, set a door at the further end of the hall swinging and creaking on its rusty hinges, and threatened to extinguish the light of a thin candle in a battered brass candlestick which stood on the last step of the staircase ready for Arthur to light himself to bed. There was no use in attempting to ascend noiselessly, every crazy plank groaned under even the most careful step, and the wide carpetless passages had

nooks and alcoves which repeated each sound till the
ear was weary of hearing it. Arthur ascended two
flights, and entered a large low room which had once
been his nursery, then his play-room, and which now
looked more like a chemist's laboratory than anything
else. The tables were heaped up with retorts, cru-
cibles, and strangely shaped glass vessels. One corner
of the room was strewn with specimens of different
varieties of ironstone, and before the rusty grate,
where no fire had been lighted for years, stood a small
furnace and a pair o bellows. As Arthur entered, he
heard the sound of shuffling feet retreating to the
further end of the room, and then a noise of something
heavy being cautiously placed on the floor. His heart
sank ; he knew very well the meaning of these sounds :
he had heard them often before. His grandfather had
a habit of coming into his room when he was absent
and stealthily removing the wood and charcoal he kept
there to feed his furnaces. The poor old man could
not reconcile himself to seeing such reckless waste of
the precious fuel he economised so painfully in his own
part of the house ; and he occasioned Arthur endless
trouble by stealing and hiding away his store as often
as he procured a fresh supply. He had heard Arthur
coming up the stairs, and, afraid of being deprived of

his bundle, he was hiding it in a dark corner, intending to come and take it away in the morning when his grandson had left the house.

Arthur walked to the middle of the room, and placed his candle on the table without speaking. It cost him a struggle to make up his mind to address his grandfather with the gentleness he always used in speaking to him; but when he looked up, and saw the old man creeping towards him from a dark corner of the room with bent, shivering figure, and pinched face whose usual perplexed expression was changed to one of fear; his annoyance gave place to a feeling of deep pity.

"You ought not to be up so late on such a cold night," he said, kindly; "let me light you back to your own room."

"Yes, it is very cold, my dear boy," the old man said, coming close up to him, and putting a thin hand on his arm, "very cold, but we can't afford fires to warm ourselves by. Wood and coal are very dear this year, dearer than ever, and you know you have promised me not to waste them. It's wicked to waste, and dangerous too; for all the people in the town say I've ruined them; and if they thought I had any money to spare—that I was hiding any, they would be so angry that they would be ready to take my life. You know that it's only a very

few pounds I have, Arthur, and you won't do anything
to give them an excuse for taking it away."

It was the old story, the painful, incoherent story
which Arthur had to hear over and over again every
day of his life. He listened to it patiently once more,
as he helped the old man across the passage to his own
room, and before he left him for the night he soothed his
mind by complying with a request he had been urging
for several days, and which Arthur had hitherto managed
to evade. The request was that Arthur should call on
a certain Mr. Serle, to whom Mr. Yonge had long ago
lent a few hundred pounds, and from whom he expected
a certain yearly interest. The money of late years had
not been regularly paid, and Mr. Yonge was in the
habit of sending Arthur pretty frequently to remind
his creditor of the omission. Arthur disliked the
errand extremely, and though he could not refuse his
grandfather's pitiful entreaties that he would try once
more to get the money, he reserved to himself the right
of saying as much or as little about the debt as he saw
fit, when old Mr. Serle and he once more talked the
matter over together.

CHAPTER III.

I watched and waited with a steadfast will :
And though the object seemed to flee away
That I so longed for, ever day by day
I watched and waited still.

Christina Rossetti.

ABOUT a week after Clemency's birthday, Mrs. Edgecombe called at Miss Arnays' house and insisted on carrying off her goddaughter to spend a few days at Combe. Clemency demurred about leaving home, for her aunt had lately been rather more unwell than usual; but Mrs. Edgecombe was in a peremptory mood, and would hear no excuses.

" I won't be called your godmother any longer," she said, " if I am not to have some authority, and may not compel you to come to me against your will now and then."

As Miss Arnays sided with her friend, Clemency was obliged to yield, and in less than half an hour she found herself seated opposite Mrs. Edgecombe in the carriage, bowling along the hard, frozen road.

"I feel better now I have secured a fresh person to tyrannise over," Mrs. Edgecombe said, smiling. "You will have a terrible time with me during the next few days; a strange restlessness has taken possession of me. I can't bear to be alone, and I can't bear to see any one a bit more tranquil than myself. I have driven my servants about till they are on the verge of rebellion, and now I have recourse to my goddaughters. I pity myself and my friends if this is to go on till the end of the month,—three weeks more, Clemency; and how many windy nights between this and then!"

" Aunt Bessie thought of you last night when the wind rose, but I persuaded her you would not be anxious. The weather is not the same all over the world ; it may have been as calm as possible last night where your son's ship was."

"Don't reason; I told you I was unreasonable; and now I forbid myself and you the most distant allusion to ships, storms, or travellers. We are going to occupy ourselves vigorously all day, and I expect you to enter with spirit into all my schemes. You know we have the birthday presents to buy. I am going to call for my second goddaughter, Sydney Serle, and take you both to the jeweller's shop at Helmsey Market to choose your presents."

"I am glad we are going to call on the Serles," Clemency answered. "I admire my pretty godsister very much. I wish she would let me know her better. We make violent efforts to be intimate when we meet in your company, but our friendship always dwindles and dies out when we are left to ourselves."

"She says it is your fault—that she is afraid of you."

"I wish she would not say so. I can't believe in any one's being afraid of me."

"I can. While you say exactly what you your- self think, and let your scorn of other people's small insincerities flash out of your eyes, girls with a great deal of sham and tinsel about them, like poor little Sydney, will always be afraid of you."

"She has more reason to be afraid of you. I should not have called her insincere."

"Did I? I don't think I meant to bring quite such a serious charge against her. By-and-by I mean to take her in hand, and cure her of her little affectations and missish ways. Her poor mother was a very superior person. She was my governess till she married Mr. Serle, and I was very fond of her; that is how Sydney comes to be my goddaughter and namesake."

"I have often wondered how it was; for you don't seem to like the other members of her family."

"I have a great respect for old Mr. Serle; he is a gentleman, though he has failed to make his son one. He is one of those morbidly shy, timid people, who take as much pains to keep down in the world as others do to struggle up. He is quite out of place among the pushing Tunstall folk. My father and Mr. Edgecombe always tried to uphold the Serles because they really are an old county family; but it was of no use: they would sink, and now George Serle is no better educated or more gentlemanlike than any ordinary tenant farmer, and Manor Combe is just like any other farmhouse."

"It is a beautiful old place, though," said Clemency. "I don't know what could be better than a farmhouse such as it is. I used to go there often when I was a child with my aunt and Rolla, and I have visions still of the delicious cool dairy, and of the orchard behind the house, and the stream at the bottom of the garden where Sydney and Rolla caught perch. I thought Sydney the happiest being on the earth then, and I have not quite left off envying her yet. I think she has a sort of fairy charm about her which wins everybody's heart. You talk of her missish ways; I think them so pretty. I can never take my eyes from her when she is in the room.

If she had been well brought up, and had not lived

always with such people as her brother George and that terrible wife of his, she might have been very charming. Some day, when my son is married, and I begin to find myself in the way at Combe, I shall travel for a year or so, and take little Sydney with me. I shall be very fond of her when I have separated her from all her relations and friends.

"Will she go with you? I would not, on such terms. And will her old father, who dotes on her so, spare her?"

"To me?—yes. And she will be glad to go—no fear of that. My only fear is that she will marry some one meanwhile. There is no one in the neighbourhood I can bear to think of her having, except—yes—your aunt's paragon, Arthur Yonge. That might do. He is good enough for foolish little Sydney; and being such a very sensible, studious young man, he will naturally want a silly wife. I would ease my conscience for past neglect by giving Sydney a fortune; and, as Mr. Serle is said to be very much in the old miser's debt, arrangements might be made that would suit all parties. I declare it is a very pretty castle in the air. What do you mean by sneering at it, Miss Franklyn?"

"I did not sneer. I was only wondering whether Sydney would be obliged to you for planning, first, to separate her from all her friends, and then to marry her *just* that you might ease your conscience by giving her a fortune."

"Now what an ungracious speech! Let me tell you that if Sydney had been sitting opposite to me instead of you, and I had spoken to her of giving you a fortune, she would have been lost in astonishment at my goodness. Her great brown eyes would have opened so wide, and conveyed all manner of flattering things to me. It is strange I don't love her the best; for of my two god-daughters she is by far the most complacent companion. Here we are, at the gate of Combe Manor. She will not keep me waiting, as you did. I have no doubt she has been sitting in her very best bonnet this half hour."

A short drive down a gravelled road brought them to the door of a many-gabled red-brick house, which, in summer time, must have been almost lost in the leaves of the rose-trees and vines whose bare arms now clasped it round. The front door opening showed a glimpse of a large, bare, untidy hall, where several children were playing, and then a very pretty young girl and a handsome grey-haired old man issued from one of the rooms and hastened down the steps to the carriage. There were some very urgent entreaties to Mrs. Edgecombe to enter the house, which she managed to decline without seeming ungracious, and then the old gentleman handed his daughter into the carriage with such loving anxious care, and such eager hopes that she would enjoy the drive, as gave Clemency a very pretty picture of the affection subsising between the two. Mrs. Edgecombe was right about the very best bonnet: Sydney was somewhat overdressed for the occasion; but the face that looked up from under the flowers and velvet was so fresh and blooming, so radiant with childishly happy smiles, that even misplaced finery could not make it otherwise than charming. So at least Clemency thought as often as the wide-opened brown eyes were turned on her, and then hastily withdrawn with the gesture of a spoilt child—too shy to be at ease when noticed, and too self-conscious to be happy when over-looked. The drive to Hemsley occupied an hour, and long before it was over Sydney recovered from her shy fit sufficiently to chatter very confidentially with her dear Mrs. Edgecombe. She had a store of little histories to relate which she had evidently been hoarding for months to pour out on the first favourable occasion —clever speeches of the children's, witticisms of her brother George's, and unkind actions of which her sister-in-law had been guilty towards herself or her father. Clemency could not quite excuse the eagerness with which these last were detailed, or the triumphant tone of the unvarying final sentence, " Yes, I let Lizzie know that I would just tell you." When she looked at the speaker's smiling lips however, and into the dancing eyes where no shade of trouble lingered, she convinced herself that her resentment could not lie very deep, and was not very formidable in its nature.

Through all Sydney's chatter the most prominent sentiment was unbounded love and admiration for her godmother ; it was perhaps a little too openly shown, but no one could doubt the reality of the feeling.

" I could not make so much of any one," Clemency said to herself; " but it is very pretty to see Sydney doing it; and Mrs. Edgecombe is more pleased with her homage than she quite knows herself."

Mrs. Edgecombe, perhaps, read the dawning of this thought in Clemency's transparent face, and being at bottom a little ashamed of allowing herself to be so openly praised, she took an opportunity, when they were in the jeweller's shop and Sydney was absorbed in turning over its treasures, to open her mind to her favourite.

" Poor little thing," she said, with a slight shrug of her shoulders, glancing towards Sydney. " She is very silly and school-girlish : but there is something lovable about her after all."

Clemency's blue eyes gave out a little indignant spark.

" Now that is too bad, Mrs. Edgecombe, when she trusts you so thoroughly. I won't have you shrug your shoulders over her for loving you."

" Well, I believe she does love me in her way; and I have just put her affection to a test worthy of it. I have told her I can only allow her one quarter of an hour to make her choice among those necklaces, and I think, from pure love of me, she will tear herself from the case in time."

" I won't have a present at all," cried Clemency. " You are so cynical to-day that I had rather not have anything to remind me of you."

" You have no choice in the matter. It is my duty as your godmother to educate you up to a feminine appreciation of baubles. You will have to stand by and take a lesson in good taste while I choose for you."

Sydney's decision was made first; it was Clemency after all who detained the party by the persistence with which she urged Mrs. Edgecombe to exchange the trinket chosen for her for a colour-box she had examined meanwhile. There were other shops to visit, and finally the library; so that the short winter's day was closing when they drove from the town. All day Clemency had noticed an unusual restlessness about her friend : she had hurried them from place to place without apparent motive, and seemed uneasy everywhere. When the horses' heads were turned homewards a change came over her mood. She leaned back listlessly and sighed.

"Pull the check-string and tell the coachman not to drive so fast," she said to Sydney. "What is he thinking of? We are none of us in any haste to get home."

"I dare say he and the horses are," said Clemency, laughing; "but, dear Mrs. Edgecombe, why do you sigh so? What ails you just now?"

"It ails me, that I have come to my senses again," she answered. "I really did not know I was still such an idiot—such a slave to my own fancies. I find I am no wiser than I was twenty years ago; the instant I begin to have a hope in life again, my old unreason comes back. Ever since I left Combe this morning I have felt as if I had an object in hurrying back there. How often I have made myself impatient in the same manner in old times when there were many joyful surprises I *could* have. How often I have filled the house with faces I was longing to see, just to find it emptier than ever when I got back to it!"

The remark was addressed to Clemency. Sydney, who had appeared wholly occupied in putting up the carriage window, startled Mrs. Edgecombe by answering with a fuller understanding of its meaning than was expected from her:—

"It is only waiting a little longer," she said, "you know, dear Mrs. Edgecombe; he will come back in time, and then the house will never be empty to you again."

Her brown eyes glistened as she spoke with tearful earnestness, the colour flew into her face, and she looked so pretty and affectionate that Clemency wondered her sympathy was not more warmly responded to. Mrs. Edgecombe did not shake off the soft little hand placed caressingly on her arm, but she drew further back into her corner of the carriage, and answered, coldly,

"You take my nonsense too literally, my dear child. Of course I do not really expect to find Colonel Edgecombe at home this evening; and when he does return, I shall not wish him to bury himself at Combe for my sake. He will, of course, be much sought after; other people have claims as well as I; and I shall not expect him to find Combe society very much to his taste. How should it be? Are they taking the turn to Manor

Combe? Pull the check-string again. I will keep you to dine with me and send you home later."

Sydney's thanks were not quite as ready as usual, and the rest of the drive was performed in silence.

"Any letters come for me—any one been here?" Mrs. Edgecombe asked eagerly of the servant who opened the door for her, when they arrived at Combe.

"No one has called, and there have been no letters," was the matter-of-fact reply.

"By the way there could not have been—there is no second post to-day," Mrs. Edgecombe observed carelessly to Clemency, as they crossed the hall together; but nevertheless there was an expression of blank disappointment on her face as she spoke. She seemed unable to shake off the feeling all the evening. She was by turns restless and weary; now getting up eagerly to make some change in the position of the books or ornaments on the drawing-room table, and before she had finished, throwing herself back listlessly on the sofa again. Clemency proposed reading aloud to her, and for a short time her voice seemed to have a soothing effect. Mrs. Edgecombe lay still, with her eyes shut. Before long, however, she sprang up, breaking into the middle of a sentence.

"What a very still night it is. I think there cannot

be a breath of wind stirring. The conservatory doors are open to the garden ; I should hear if there were any wind."

"Do you always have the doors left open these cold nights, that you may listen to the wind?" said Clemency. "Dear Mrs. Edgecombe, I did not know you had such an over-anxious heart. If Aunt Bessie had a friend at sea, I doubt whether even she would have thought of doing that."

"If she had had a son at sea she would."

"But ——"

"Well go on. You know I choose that you should always speak out whatever is in your mind to me."

"It is hardly right to say it, but till lately I used not to think you cared so *very* much for your son. Till lately you always spoke with a sort of indifference about his being away, and though I was quite a child when he lived at Combe, I used to fancy that there was a strange coldness and reserve in your manner to him then."

"No, not coldness."

"Restraint, then ; as if you were both half afraid of what you might say to each other."

"We were afraid—each afraid of bringing trouble on the other by showing natural affection. Oh, it was a bitter bondage, but he never misunderstood me. For years after he left me I was not *indifferent* to his absence, but so glad to know that he was free, and that I was bearing the petty, wearing, hourly contradictions alone. Of late years, I have smothered my longing to see him from fear of his injuring his prospects or reputation by hurrying home to gratify me. But now that the desire, so long crushed down, has had free way, it has grown up, like Jonah's gourd, in one night, to overshadow every other feeling. My whole soul has gone into it. Hark! is there not some sound outside? Is it a step, or the creaking of a bough? Can the wind be rising again?"

"Dear Mrs. Edgecombe, no, there is not a breath stirring. Do take advantage of this still night to be at rest for once."

"Only I don't like such perfect stillness coming after a storm; to my fancy there is something ominous in it. It is as if the wind rested because it had done its work, and was awed into quiet by remorse for the mischief it had done."

"I suppose it is having an over-strong wish that has made you so ingenious in self-torture."

"Now Clemency, that remark savours of your aunt's philosophy, and I will not have it. If a wish is not

wrong, why not put one's whole heart into it. I have
been petrified long enough ; I will not have the returning life chilled out of me by being persuaded that torpor
is the higher state ; I won't talk to you any more.
You are not such a comfortable companion as Sydney,
when one is in a thoroughly unreasonable state of mind.
I can be cross and whimsical at my ease with her ; she
never presumes to think I can be wrong. Let her read
to me now. I shall not listen ; but she will not look up
reproachfully now and then, as if she thought I ought
to control myself and attend."

Clemency protested that she had not had any such
thought while she had been reading ; but she was
not sorry to resign her post to Sydney, who was all
eagerness to take it. An hour, which she might spend
quite as she pleased at Combe, was always a treat to
her, especially if it came in the evening of a busy day.
She enjoyed wandering through the lonely rooms, and
the wide marble-pillared hall, when the dim light gave
an almost solemn character to the stately antique furniture with which old Mr. Edgecombe's taste had filled
them. She was usually too much occupied with her
own thoughts to give conscious heed to the objects
round her ; yet the flickering fire-light bringing out
suddenly every now and then some grotesque form or

lovely face in the oak carving, the mysterious shadows,
the marbles looking down with calm faces from their
niches, the reflected glow on quaintly-framed mirror
and painted ceiling, were not wholly lost upon her.
Unconsciously they gave a colour to her thoughts, and
created round her a perfect atmosphere for dreaming in.
The drawing-room, where Mrs. Edgecombe and Sydney
sat, opened into a library, and there Clemency generally
betook herself when she had visited all her favourite
haunts.   There was a conservatory at the end opening
on the garden, and the doors, by Mrs. Edgecombe's
orders, were left open.   The night was so still that the
lamps hanging from the roof burned steadily, showing
the broad green 'and crimson leaves of tropical plants,
tree ferns, bananas, and palm fronds, which were all
its winter state had to show.

Clemency was tempted to enter and transport herself,
by the help of the green leaves and faint fragrance, to
the summer of another hemisphere. When she had taken
a turn or two, it struck her that the cold wintry light of
the full moon streaming through the roof, gave a strange
unreal appearance to the rich velvet green leaves she
was moving among. A wizard, she thought, might have
called up such a phantom vision of summer in a frozen
land. She remembered a quaint story in Marco Polo's

travels of the performance of some such feat. To rid
herself of the impression, she opened a door at the
further end of the conservatory, and stepped out to see
how the snow-covered garden and the moonlight agreed
together. Once out, even the chill air did not dispose
her to satisfy herself soon with gazing. It was almost
as light as day, but she found the same phantom-like
aspect there too. The snowy ground reflected the moon-
beams in patches of dazzling white, the shadows of the
shrubs lay upon it, distinct, black and motionless, while
the great trees at the bottom of the garden stood round
like a close ranged army of dark indistinct gigantic
forms, uniting the cold pale sky and the white silent
earth. After long gazing abroad, Clemency's eyes
rested on the shadow of one particular shrub, growing
not far from her on the slope of the lawn. Half unconsciously she traced the outline of each pointed leaf, and
matched it with the form of the tree. The topmost
bough puzzled her; it was rounder than the others,
and it had a tremulous motion when all else was still.
To satisfy her curiosity, she caught up a shawl hanging behind the door, wrapped it round her and ran
lightly down the steps on to the lawn. There she
found herself too much in the shadow of the tree to
see anything, but she stopped to gather a bough of

arbutus laden with crimson fruit, which hung tempt-
ingly near her hand ; then to stare up at Orion directly
above her head, hanging so low that she thought it
must have been on such a winter's night as this that
Wordsworth's idiot boy " hoped to catch a star, and in
his pocket bring it home."

It was a minute or two before she turned to remount
the steps. A figure stood at the top as motionless as
everything else that night. A feeling of superstitious
awe held her still for one minute, the next, surprise and
fear passed away in eager hope. She bounded up the
steps, stood before the stranger, and looked eagerly,
frankly up into his face.

"It is you, then, Colonel Edgecombe ; you are come,"
she said, holding out a welcoming hand. No likeness
to his mother guided her to certainty, only a dim recollection that she had seen the face that confronted
her before, when the regular features were less sun-
burnt, and the dark eyes and heavily marked brows
less imposing than they were now. It did not embarrass
her, however, in the least to have those great eyes looking straight down into hers, she only saw that there
was a trouble in them, with which she could sympathise.

"Am I expected, then ?" he asked in the same
breathless tone in which she had spoken ; " surely I

cannot be. I travelled night and day lest the news of the disaster to our ship should reach her before I did."

"She has heard nothing ; she does not really expect you till the next mail is due."

"Ah, then she has missed a letter. My departure from India was hastened. I ought to have been here three days ago. Is she here, and well ?"

"Yes, quite well ; in the drawing-room now."

" Thank God !"

Clemency felt disposed to put out her hand again for another welcoming shake, such warm pleasure did the earnest tone in which these words were uttered send to her heart. She augured from them that her aunt's forebodings were clearly wrong, and that her friend was going to be as happy as she expected. As they walked down the conservatory Colonel Edgecombe spoke again in a low voice,—

"I walked here from the little Combe station," he said, "and took the short cut through the woods. For the last ten minutes I have been prowling about the garden, hoping to see some servant I knew whom I could trust to tell my mother. I dreaded hearing she was ill or from home. How came *you* to be expecting me, as you had not had my letter ? "

" Oh, we have always been expecting you, ever since

we heard that there was a chance of your coming," Clemency answered, simply. "But the drawing-room door is open; had I not better go in first?"

"Yes do; but stay one moment, I must look."

They were now in the dining-room, the fire had sunk low and it was almost dark there, but the open doorway beyond, framed as in a picture, the figures of Mrs. Edgecombe, half-reclining on the sofa, and Sydney Serle sitting on a low stool at her feet.

Sydney had paused in her reading to ask a question, and she was now looking up waiting for the answer, with her very prettiest wondering expression in her large brown eyes. They could see the amused smile that parted Mrs. Edgecombe's lips as she roused herself to answer. Clemency and her companion gazed silently, till Mrs. Edgecombe sank back on the sofa, and Sydney's eyes turned again on her book; then they exchanged an understanding glance. Clemency felt rather than saw that her sympathy and comprehension were taken for granted.

"Now go in and prepare her to see me," Colonel Edgecombe said. "I am satisfied, she is less altered than I feared she might be. Who is that sitting by her?"

"Sydney Serle."

"Impossible! Little Sydney Serle! She was quite a child when I went away; she can't have grown up like that."

The tone was a little raised, and Mrs. Edgecombe once more sprang up on the sofa. Her face grew eager, and her eyes strained into the darkness.

"Clemency, is that you? Come here!"

Clemency felt her limbs tremble a little as she walked, and she knew that it would be vain to try to command her countenance; her beaming eyes and flushed cheek would perhaps best tell their own tale. One glance at them was enough for Mrs. Edgecombe.

"He is come," she said, "I know; no need to keep me waiting." And the next instant she was in her son's arms, and Clemency beckoned the astonished Sydney to follow her out of the room. Then she had to explain more clearly the events of the evening; and the servants, who had discovered somehow that something unusual was going on, flocked into the hall and crowded round her to hear the news again and again from her lips. She was simply amused to find herself raised to a temporary position of importance in the house from being the favoured person who could testify to the actual presence of its master, and it gave her pleasure to witness such hearty rejoicing. Sydney, on

the other hand, seemed to lose sympathy with Mrs.
Edgecombe, in the nervous fidgety anxiety that seized
her, lest she should be in the way, or seem to take upon
herself more share in the general joy than she was
entitled to.

"Do let me go home at once," she implored
Clemency. " Mrs. Edgecombe won't think of me again,
I am sure she won't. And for me to see Colonel
Edgecombe the first evening of his arrival before other
people see him—oh, it could not be thought of."

"Why not?" asked Clemency, laughing. "I have
seen him, and it has not done me any harm. You were
always his favourite when we were children, you know;
and he remembered your name perfectly."

"Did he really; he used to be very good to me. Of
course I remember; but now it is so different; and,
indeed—indeed—I had rather go home. Mrs. Edgecombe won't see me again to-night. Do please manage
to have the carriage brought round for me at once."

Her agitation and scruples struck Clemency as very
incomprehensible and missish, but as she saw that her
discomfort was real, she contrived to have her wish
attended to, and saw her drive from the front-door just
as Mrs. Edgecombe, leaning proudly on her son's arm,
emerged from the drawing-room to speak to the servants

assembled in the hall. In the shade of one of the
pillars, Clemency watched the greetings, the hearty
hand-shakings, the tearful, almost adoring looks with
which the returned wanderer was received. It was not an
ordinary home-coming. Few of the servants assembled
had not experienced something of the petty domestic
tyranny that had driven the heir early from his home.
They had secretly sympathised with his rebellion against
it. They had wept over his mother's desolation when he
had left her, and now that he had returned with a little
aura of fame hanging round him, which in their eyes
raised him to the position of a hero, they hardly knew
how to give him honour or welcome enough. Clemency
felt a reflection of the general enthusiasm ; the sight of
the proud triumph in Mrs. Edgecombe's face woke a
corresponding glow in her own heart. There was a
little lurking ambition in her character which had
never hitherto found any vent. She had had vague
longings for some beautiful gift or distinction which
would make life look glorious and worthy to her. That
night she felt as if she had suddenly discovered the true
object towards which a woman's ambition turns. To
see those she loves honoured, to be loved by those who
are worthy of honour ; in the light of that glory she felt
she should like to move. It was *that* she had been

unconsciously coveting all this time. How heartily she sympathised with her friend in having gained it. When the servants began to move away, Clemency retired again into the library, and began once more to pace up and down, this time to calm the flutter of her spirits, and to think out the new thought that had come to her. Would her only dearly-loved brother Rolla ever enjoy such a home-coming as this of Colonel Edge-combe's ? She tried to fancy it, she counted up the various proofs of talent he had given, and recalled his winning manners and occasional flashes of generous feeling. It would not do ; loveable Rolla would always be, but she could not fancy such a change as that the thought of him would bring any sensation to her heart but tender anxiety, and the instinct of protection. Then she almost hated herself for wishing a change in their relationship to each other. Had it not been the great object of her life ever since she could remember to stand between Rolla and every annoyance, trouble, or harm that threatened to come near him? No, she would not be ambitious for Rolla ; to know that he was safe and happy was such an immense boon, she would not venture to wish anything else. It was some time before she had any interruption to these thoughts, for it was long after the usual bedtime when

Mrs. Edgecombe came into the library to look for her.

"There is no need to apologise to you for leaving you alone so long," she said, smiling.

"No need, indeed," cried Clemency; "I have only been waiting up to tell you how happy I am."

"Thank you, Clemency. I will tell you something; you are the only person in the world to whom I should not have grudged the pleasure of having seen him first, I am so glad you brought him to me."

"I too am glad that I was here. I would not have missed seeing your face in the hall to-night for anything. I know now what Aunt Bessie means by talking about how you looked in the days when you were happy."

"She will see me look happy again; dear, dear Bessie, we shall astonish her out of her melancholy philosophy. It is all better than I expected. He has been talking to me, Clemency, just this once of our old sorrows, that the pain of them may be healed for ever. I know exactly now why he went away, and how he longed to confide in me, and could not for fear of bringing trouble on me. It was just here that he wished me good-night the last time, with a perfectly unconcerned face, but he tells me he stood for two hours at the door of my room before he left early the next morning. I confess it has always been a thorn in my heart that he could go without confiding in me, now he has taken it out. I am satisfied."

" I wonder——"

" Why do you pause, Clemency? surely you have never thought he ought not to have gone at all."

" Dear Mrs. Edgecombe," said Clemency, laughing, " I don't know that I ever presumed quite so far as that ; but I have sometimes thought that Arthur Yonge would not have gone under the same circumstances."

" Arthur Yonge ! But how can you compare the two ? How should Arthur Yonge have the same sensibility, the same quick sense of honour ? It would be absurd indeed to judge my son by such a standard."

" We won't dispute to-night; but you know I don't subscribe to your belief that all fine feelings are confined to the county families. I think townspeople have them too, sometimes. Here is Colonel Edgecombe coming to look for you. I will say good-night, and keep my curiosity to know about the shipwreck till to-morrow morning."

" He shall tell you himself at breakfast-time; but just this you shall let me say to-night. Was it not strange that I should have known it, that I should have felt all I did in that storm ?"

"Only unluckily it was not the right storm. Mother," said Colonel Edgecombe, who was now standing near them, looking down from his great height on his mother's face, with a half-mocking, half-admiring smile, " I am afraid I can't let you make a romance about it; the *Panther* was wrecked in the Red Sea more than a fortnight ago, before you got my letter, when you were not dreaming of storms."

" Ah, but storms travel ; it had to cross Europe, and it came and blew its tale against my window last night. I am certain of it, Walter.   It is useless for you to contradict me."

He put his arm round her waist and drew her towards him, then looked laughingly across at Clemency.   " She is not a bit altered, this mother of mine, Miss Franklyn ; she still loves the last word, and is as ingenious as ever in inventing monstrous reasons to prove that she is always right.   What trouble I shall have with her !"

"And I with you.   Clemency, you and I shall never have another hour's sensible talk ; he will always come in and spoil everything with his silly banter.   He knows how I hate it."

Clemency perceived that the two had fallen at once into the same playful exaggerating tone of conversation that used to puzzle her when she was a grave, literal-minded child. She was not sure that she should be able to sustain a part in it any better now, but she had no doubt about the extreme pleasure it gave her friend to find herself talking in the old strain once more.

As they were leaving the room together, Colonel Edgecombe glanced round. "But surely you had another guest?" he said.

"Sydney Serle," cried Mrs. Edgecombe; "I had forgotten all about her. I hope you looked after her, Clemency. I hope she went home just when she pleased."

Clemency explained that Sydney had refrained from wishing Mrs. Edgecombe good-night for fear of disturbing her.

"How sensible of the little thing," said Mrs. Edgecombe. "Yes, she was quite right. I like her for it. I think I will drive over and see her to-morrow."

"And you shall take me with you," the Colonel exclaimed. "I am in a hurry to visit all my old haunts. How often I have pictured to myself, on hot days in India, that orchard at Manor Combe, with the little river running through it!"

"Well, we will see. I don't know that I shall let you call on the Serles the very day after your arrival. It would be so cruel to Mrs. George. She would never know how to give herself airs enough afterwards; and really she is sufficiently puzzled on that head as it is."

"But I hope you will let me go somewhere. I am not prepared to stay at home till you have discovered an acquaintance strong-minded enough to survive the honour of seeing me. Miss Franklyn, is it not fortunate that I early learned to disbelieve every word my mother says, and that her insinuations about my consequence only mortify me?" Colonel Edgecombe looked towards Clemency, but she had preceded them up the great staircase, and was nearly out of hearing.

Mrs. Edgecombe saw that his eyes followed her retreating figure till a turn in the passage hid it, and she could not help putting into words the expression she thought she read in them.

"Is not she beautiful?" she said. "Are you not rather surprised? I don't suppose you have seen any-one so beautiful since you left England?"

"Perhaps not; but she is not so beautiful as you are, mother. No one is—that is my creed; and I am in no haste to change it. When I am asked how I escape falling in love, I always answer, because I have never seen anyone to be compared to my mother. Miss Franklyn will never sweep up and down stairs as grandly as you do."

Mrs. Edgecombe was satisfied; the one little scrap of information she was still anxious for had been given, and she retired to her room with her cup of happiness overflowingly full. Her son had come back safe, and like his old self, and he had no story of an unknown rival in his heart to reveal to her on the morrow. She might build what castles in the air she chose, and paint out the bright future in the colours that best pleased her.

For the first time in her life she confessed herself perfectly happy, and as she was not given to self-inspection, she did not ask how it was that the thought awoke rather a feeling of triumph than one of thankfulness in her heart. She felt that the brightness now dawning on her life had been patiently waited for, long worked for, skilfully planned; it depended on herself, she thought, to enjoy it thoroughly, and hold it fast.

CHAPTER IV.

From this fair point of present bliss,
  Where we together stand,
Let me look back once more, and trace
  That long and desert land,
Wherein till now was cast my lot,
And I could live, and thou wert not.
                                A. A. Proctor.

LONG before Clemency rose the next morning, in the first waking moment, when her eyes fell on the well-known furniture of her room at High Combe, she had a consciousness of some very great event having happened in the household, and of everything around her being changed. The heavy bed cornices, the polished oak presses, the china and ancient blue delf loomed through the faint wintry morning light as large and imposing as ever; but the grotesque faces that Clemency was wont to trace in them wore quite a new aspect, and told her a different story from any she had ever heard from them before. "We have been waiting," they seemed to her to say, "waiting so many years, and now something has happened, the

sound of it has reached us, and we are opening our
eyes and beginning to live again." As the light crept
into the room, the fantastic faces resolved themselves
into spots and lines, but the sense of strangeness only
deepened in Clemency's mind. She lay listening to
unwonted noises, quick steps passing backwards and
forwards, hasty slamming of doors, whispering and
laughing in far-off passages. It seemed that a new
pulse of life was beating in the solemn, silent old
house, and that the very walls and ceiling throbbed
and tingled with it.

Before she left her room, she had a visit from the
old housekeeper, who had a special affection for Clemency, and now sought her for the express purpose of
being the first to inform her that the Colonel had been
up long before daylight; that he had visited every
room in the house, and the stables, and that now he had
walked down to the East Lodge, to see a superannuated
coachman, who was bedridden there. "It was as like
old times as could be," she went on, making a pretext
of smoothing out the trimming of Clemency's dress to
secure her as a listener. "So like old times; to think
of his remembering about the old stable lantern I used
to keep for him in my room, and insisting on using it
this morning; and of his putting me in mind of the

times when I used to make him a hot cup of tea, and
insist on his drinking it before he set off on his early
winter morning ride. He was always the one to be up
early, summer and winter, and have his sport or his gallop,
or carry on his devices, whatever they might be, before
—well, before—his father, the old master—was up,
to make us all afraid of speaking above our breath.
He was a terrible man was old Mr. Edgecombe, a terribly bad-tempered man. You remember him enough
to know that, my dear Miss Franklyn; but there's no
one but myself, I often think, that knows all my poor
dear mistress has had to suffer from him."

"I remember Mr. Edgecombe quite well," Clemency
answered, quietly; and then she turned the conversation
back to the joyful event of yesterday, for her aunt had
often warned her against being drawn on to discuss the
late Mr. Edgecombe's character with any of the old
servants of the house.

The brightness that pervaded the whole house struck
her afresh as she ran downstairs and came into the
front hall. There was a fire burning on the hearth.
She had never seen one there before, or imagined that
the polished brass dogs could be put to any use. And
through the wide-open front door a flood of pale, wintry
sunshine streamed in, putting out the reflection of the

fire on the chequered marble pavement, but leaving the
dark spaces behind the pillars and the armour on the
walls to rejoice in its ruddy glow. Some one had
swept the snow from the steps leading down into the
garden, and scattered a plentiful meal for the birds
there. A flock of sparrows and chaffinches, and a
robin redbreast were enjoying it, and filling the frosty
air with quick shrill chirps and fragments of song.
In the moment during which Clemency paused to
listen to them, a new sound came suddenly down and
shivered their morning concert ; it was the sweet clash
of the village church bells, breaking into a joyful peal.
Nearer and nearer the wind brought the sound into
the hall, till Clemency thought the air that touched
her cheek vibrated with music ; then it moved further
off, up to the sky, away to the woods, to tell out its
good news, and back again, making a tumult of rejoicing all round her. Could this be the gloomy old
hall at High Combe ? Surely a new age of the world
had begun since yesterday ! It was with a dreamy
feeling, as if crossing the threshold might bring her
anywhere, that Clemency turned the handle of the
library door at last, and entered. The same sensation
of fresh air and brightness and joyful sounds came over
her. The aspect of the room was altogether changed

since last night; the furniture had been placed in new positions, and books taken from the shelves were scattered about on the tables. Colonel Edgecombe was standing at the open window with a book in his hand. He greeted Clemency briefly, and went on reading, while she busied herself with her usual morning task at Combe, of preparing the tea. Mrs. Edgecombe was always late in the morning, and liked to find the tea made, and Clemency ready to give it to her when she came down. It was the pleasant beginning of the day for her, which belonged to Clemency's visits only, she used to say.

By-and-by Colonel Edgecombe walked up to the table, still with the open book in his hand. "Miss Franklyn," he said, suddenly, "what lies people do tell in books, to be sure."

"Do they?" said Clemency.

"Yes; see here. My old Catechism of Natural History, which I have routed out from the back of that book-shelf, says that a robin is not a long-lived bird; and now, look at that fellow out there, does he seem any worse for his years; he's been alive ever since I can remember. I fed him on that door-step the morning I left home, and there he was waiting about for me when I came out to-day."

"Are you sure it is the same robin?" said Clemency, smiling.

"As sure as my mother was about the storm, as sure as I am that these are the identical trout-flies I shut up in this book in a hurry one autumn afternoon, little dreaming that I should go to India and back before I used them. I don't believe the book has been touched since I last shut it, nor any one of the books. The house has got to have a strangely shut-up Mausoleum kind of air, as if no one had lived in it for a hundred years or so. I have been doing my best since five o'clock this morning, to make it look like itself again."

"Unlike itself, I think; it has always looked empty and dead since I can remember it."

"And all the while I have been picturing it to myself as it used to be when I lived here, and kept up a constant active fight against all formality and state, my mother seconding me. Yet I can't understand how it has come to this. My mother must be more changed than I thought last night, if she has ceased to care how things look round her. I fear that long sorrow and solitude have crushed even her spirits; I ought to have come home sooner. The year of my father's last illness must have been a very miserable time for her."

"It was very sad. Mr. Edgecombe suffered so

terribly; and latterly he could not bear to see anyone but her. She used to be alone with him almost
always."

"But you were often here. My mother told me in
her letters what comfort she had in your visits, and how
brave and patient you were."

"I used to be allowed to sit with Mr. Edgecombe for
an hour or so sometimes while she rested, but I was not
really brave at all. I am afraid I was always very glad
when the hour was over; it is so dreadful to see a
person suffer when one can do nothing. I often wonder
now how Mrs. Edgecombe could bear to see it all day
long for so many months."

"And you wonder, too, don't you, that I let her bear
it all alone? that I did not come home while my father
was ill to help and support her?"

"No," Clemency answered. "I have never wondered
about that. I knew, of course, that you would have
come to her if it had been possible. You must have
wanted to come." She looked up rather suddenly
as she finished speaking, and was surprised to see an
expression of embarrassment and pain on Colonel
Edgecombe's face.

"Well, at all events," he said quickly, "I am glad I
am here now. The bad days for my mother are over

for ever now, and we must all do our best to make
her forget them. She shall have nothing but enjoyment
for the rest of her life, and her own way in everything.
I shall take care of that."

" It will not be difficult," Clemency answered. " Her
way will always be yours, and she will now see a reason
for taking it."

" No, no, that won't do ; there must be no question
about reasons ; she must please herself in complete
unreason. Above all I must not institute a new
tyranny. I used to abuse her boundless complaisance
to me terribly in old times. We must begin now on a
better system ; and there you must help me, Miss
Franklyn. You understand my mother better than
anyone in the world, she says ; you must instruct me in
her likes and dislikes, and scold me whenever you see
that I am growing exacting or letting her sacrifice
herself as she used to do. Why do you shake your
head ? I can see that you have pluck enough to speak
your mind openly, and besides, no one ever is really
afraid of me."

Clemency glanced up into his face ; the dark brows
looked as if they could be drawn fiercely together, and
the black eyes, just then full of frank sweetness, were
clearly capable of a very different expression ; and yet

from the bottom of her heart she could answer as frankly as he had asked. " No, I should not be afraid of you. I am never afraid of Mrs. Edgecombe, though most people say they are."

" That's right ; well, it's a bargain between us, is it not ? And now I shall feel conscience free. I shall indulge myself in all sorts of whims, and leave it to you to pull me up short when I grow troublesome to other people. How happy we are going to be. Ah ! there she is. Now, Miss Franklyn, is not that worth coming all the way from India to see ?"

Clemency thought it was, when turning round she caught Mrs. Edgecombe's start of surprise as she entered the changed room, and then the glow of pleasure that lighted up her whole face. Instead of going forward to meet her, Colonel Edgecombe sat down, rubbed his hands together, and laughed a low laugh of pleasure by way of greeting. Mrs. Edgecombe just laid her hand on his head in passing. " You absurd boy," she said ; and then Clemency had the two outstretched hands given to her, and the tenderest kiss Mrs. Edgecombe had ever bestowed, pressed on her forehead.

" Now, mother, take your proper place and give me some tea," her son said. " I have been up four hours, and I am ravenously hungry."

"This is my place," Mrs. Edgecombe answered, drawing a chair to the fire. "Do you suppose I trouble
myself to dispense tea when Clemency is here to do it
better for me? I am an old woman now, Walter, and
like to be waited on. No, *you* are to sit still and eat;
Clemency will bring my cup to me. Do you suppose
you can move about the room as pleasantly as she can,
you great awkward creature? Be quiet and take a
lesson for future mornings, when I shall have to put up
with your services."

Clemency was remarkably free from the self-conscious-
ness that makes observation embarrassing, or she would
have found the breakfast-hour rather a trying ordeal
to her nerves. Colonel Edgecombe interpreted his
mother's injunction to sit still and take a lesson in
serving very literally. He made no further offers of
help, but Clemency felt his eyes following her as she
passed backwards and forwards between the table and
the fire, and every now and then the low, soft laugh of
pleasure was heard again, at moments when, as far as
she could perceive, there was no special cause for merriment. It was better when the meal was over; the
party did not break up; but Colonel Edgecombe drew his
chair in a line with his mother's by the fire, and began
to talk. After an attempt to withdraw, and leave the

mother and son together, which Mrs. Edgecombe prevented, Clemency found a nook on the opposite side of
the fire-place where she could sit and listen, and screen
her face from the fire and from inquisitive eyes as
well. She was soon glad that Mrs. Edgecombe had
desired her to• remain, for the conversation grew very
interesting. It was a feast of talk, such as can be
enjoyed only by very intimate friends, or relations who
love each other dearly, when, after a long separation,
they first open their minds to each other—by them,
perhaps, never after the first burst of renewed confidence is over, for, by and by, the injury which long
separation does to close intimacies is apt to make
itself felt. That morning's conversation was all pure
enjoyment. Colonel Edgecombe could talk about
himself naturally and freely when there was good
reason to do so ; and Clemency found herself listening
to exciting tales of adventure, in which he had taken
part, and to descriptions of days of battle and scenes of
peril and glory, which she knew would be famous in
the world's history for ever. Colonel Edgecombe, to
gratify his present auditors, made no effort to give a
general description which any one might hear; he spoke
only of his own experience of the memorable days ; of
what he had actually seen and felt and heard, varying

his narrative, with many minute every-day details
quite personal to himself, and with recollections of odd
incongruous thoughts or trifling observations which
seemed to have come to him at the most unlikely
moments, and to remain connected in his mind for
ever with the perils through which he had passed.
Clemency wondered whether he adopted this form of
narrative to turn their attention from the prominent
part he had really taken in the great events of which
he was speaking, or whether it showed a want of
seriousness in his character. To her inexperience it
seemed so strange that a person should recall with
pleasure a trifling speech or a ridiculous accident which
occurred in the midst of peril and in the presence of
death.

The matter-of-fact tone pleased Clemency better
when Mrs. Edgecombe tried, by skilful questions, to
draw from her son an acknowledgment of the importance of his own services. He was always ready to
answer questions, but no insinuations could make him
see himself in the light of a hero, or admit that he had
done anything he could possibly have avoided doing.
He had been lucky. That was all—some people were
lucky—and the luck of being in the way when there
was anything to be done, had, he acknowledged, fallen

singularly to his share. The promised story of the shipwreck was given with the same detail and the same determination not to allow any merit to his own, or indeed
to any other person's exertions. When things had to be
done, of course some one naturally did them. Clemency
followed every word with even greater pleasure than she
had felt before. The story was more recent than any
of the others, and there was every now and then in the
speaker's words and face the touch of feeling of gratitude for present safety, and awe at past peril, which she
had hitherto missed. Mrs. Edgecombe could not be
satisfied with asking questions, yet she covered her eyes
and shuddered every now and then as if she could
hardly bear to hear. Then she made Clemency help
her to recall how she had passed the days and nights
during which her son had been drifting in an open
boat on an angry sea, in momentary peril of his life.
They discovered that the very worst time, when the last
provisions had been distributed, and hope had all but
gone, was the evening which Mrs. Edgecombe had spent
at Clemency's birthday party.

"And I was so happy that night, and so angry with
your aunt for trying to check my confidence," Mrs.
Edgecombe exclaimed. "If I had known—if I could
have seen you——"

"But you did not, dearest mother. And now consider what an admission you have made. You can never talk to Miss Franklyn or me about presentiments again. You have shown yourself woefully at fault. Now, I was much nearer seeing you. I protest on that night, just when we had divided our last biscuit, and passed round our last thimbleful of water, I had a distinct vision of you sitting by a blazing fire, drinking oceans of tea and eating scores of muffins; precisely what you were doing at that time on Miss Franklyn's birthnight; now, was it not? I think I recollect being present on one such occasion, and misbehaving myself terribly by tying the young ladies' hair-plaits together and letting off crackers under the tea-table. I seriously think now that my sufferings on the last 31st of January were a well-merited punishment for such an enormity."

There was no more grave conversation after this remark. Colonel Edgecombe insisted on having a description of the guests present at Clemency's party, and found fault with his mother's disparaging remarks on her neighbours, all of whom he professed an intention of finding delightful. The beauty of the day passed off while they sat talking. Snow-clouds gathered in the sky, and in the afternoon began to descend in slow-falling flakes. Colonel Edgecombe declared his inten-

tion of going out for a long walk, that he might have
the satisfaction of being well snowed upon once more;
and when he had gone, Clemency discovered that there
was only enough of the short day remaining to allow
her to reach Tunstall before dark, if she set out at
once.

Mrs. Edgecombe wanted to make the snow-storm an
excuse for keeping her at High Combe.

"You might let me have one quite perfect day," she
urged. "You are not like Sydney, ready to fancy
yourself superseded. You know that I shall miss you
even to-day with him beside me."

"Yes, I know," Clemency answered; "and, indeed,
dear Mrs. Edgecombe, I am grateful; but Aunt
Bessie will miss me more. You have so much brightness, you can spare a little to her. I want to brighten
her with your good news."

"Dear Aunt Bessie! Yes; she must not wait another day for it. If I could but lift her up to my
height of happiness! Yet, I dare say she would tell
me she had rather remain as she is; and declare she
had no wish to change places with me. I am afraid I
should quarrel with her contented calm if I saw her
to-day. Her still, spiritual face would strike chill upon
me like a warning. Confess you have some of the

same feeling, Clemency, that leaving this house now for hers is passing from sunshine to shadow."

"No, no! I don't feel that at all. Dear Mrs. Edgecombe, you surely don't want to make me discontented with my own home! If I found coming here did that, I would never come again."

"I shall let you go more willingly if you will confess that it is a sacrifice; that you will think just a little regretfully of me and of the new stories I shall hear to-night."

"If I say so now, I shall regret that I said it this evening when Aunt Bessie and I are together."

"That will do; you are a good girl. Your eyes tell the exact truth, even when your lips will not."

Colonel Edgecombe's ramble was prolonged till much later than he had intended when setting out, so that his mother had several solitary hours during the evening. Supposing her in earnest in her wish that Clemency should suffer for her determination to leave Combe, she would not have been gratified if she could have amused her leisure by peeping into Miss Arnays' little drawing-room and watching the faces and overhearing the brisk conversation that went on between the three people seated there.

Mrs. Franklyn had called on Miss Arnays during

the morning, and left a newspaper, which was found to contain a full account of the loss of the Panther (the vessel in which Colonel Edgecombe had sailed from India), and the narrow escape and sufferings of her passengers and crew. Colonel Edgecombe was mentioned several times in the narrative, as one of the two or three to whose presence of mind and energy in maintaining order, the escape of the survivors might be considered due. After tea Clemency took her usual seat on a footstool by her aunt's arm-chair, and began a second reading of the paragraph interspersed with additional particulars, which she had gathered from the Colonel's own lips. Before she had proceeded far she was interrupted by the entrance of Arthur Yonge, whom she had not seen since her birthday. When she remembered this, it struck her as rather strange that they should not have met for more than a fortnight; such a thing had never occurred before.

"You don't deserve that I should get up from my comfortable seat to shake hands," she said, "for I do believe you have been in a bad temper for two whole weeks. I sent you a message the day before yesterday that you were to come in and make tea for Aunt Bessie while I was away, and you did not attend to it."

"But I came in after tea and read a chapter of

'Leighton, on St. Peter,' and did my best to make myself useful."

"That was not what I asked you to do. Could not you condescend to oblige me?"

"I did not understand that you insisted on the tea-making."

"Oh, Arthur! when you know that I shall consider your giving way on this point a proof that Aunt Bessie and I have more influence with you than Mrs. Franklyn!"

"You know I don't care the least in the world what Mrs. Franklyn says about me."

"You care terribly. You keep away from us just because you can't forget a stupid little speech of hers. You have avoided eating or drinking in her house since that unlucky day when she found you here and said——"

"Don't!" cried Arthur, his whole face flushing crimson.

"And you call that not caring," said Clemency, "when you can't bear to hear the foolish words again!"

"I can't bear to hear *you* repeat an insinuation that I take advantage of your aunt's kindness to escape the discomfort of my own home; that I come here for what I can get, in fact. It amounted to that."

"But it was Mrs. Franklyn that said it," cried Clemency. "Now, Aunt Bessie, does it not show something morbid in Arthur's mind—something not quite sound in his friendship to us, when he can allow such a remark as that to rankle so long? Won't you scold him?"

"No, not now. He had a sermon last night. Let him sit down, he looks tired; and do you begin your story over again. If he is morbid, the kindest thing is to give him something fresh to think of."

Clemency recommenced the interrupted narrative; but she did not give quite such fluent explanations now that she had a second listener. Her aunt interposed a question now and then, but Arthur heard to the end without comment. If she had not observed that he really did look tired and out of spirits, she would have been very angry with his want of enthusiasm.

"What a lucky fellow Colonel Edgecombe seems to be!" Arthur remarked, when the reading came to an end.

"Just what he says himself," cried Clemency, "about the shipwreck, and about everything he has done in India."

"I never like to hear that word," Miss Arnays interposed gently; "surely he ought to speak more reverently of escape from so many dangers."

"Dear aunt! Arthur does not mean that Colonel

Edgecombe is lucky for having escaped the dangers, but for being in them. It is the luck of having been shipwrecked and half starved, and of having been wounded in two battles, that Arthur envies."

"Well, as long as such deeds and sufferings get such disproportionate sympathy and reward, one can but envy a person to whose lot they fall."

"You ought not to covet sympathy and reward that you consider disproportionate."

"I consider it cheaply earned : that is no reason for not coveting it."

"You have never paid the cost, so you don't know."

"Women never understand that there can be courage and effort, without noisy result. It is just the least costly kind that they admire."

"Despise our admiration then, since we don't know how to bestow it."

"I have just confessed that I am envious,—is not that enough ? "

"I am glad you acknowledge yourself so far human. I have no patience with people who pretend they don't care for praise. It may not be the best thing, or nearly the best, but it is very good and sweet. To know one has done something that makes everyone one meets look upon one with favour, must be a delightful feeling.

It must be like living in perpetual sunshine. Healthy, clear sunshine too, I think, in which everything generous and noble in a character must come out and flourish. Oh, if I had been a man, should I not have been ambitious; and you would have been a great cross to me, Aunt Bessie, for you would never have sympathised. If I had come back famous from India to you, you would not have been as proud of me as Mrs. Edgecombe is of her son."

Clemency turned a glowing eager face up to her aunt as she spoke, but she did not get an immediate answer. A sudden impatient movement of Arthur's brought the fire-irons down on the guard with a clatter too distressing to Miss Arnays' nerves to be recovered all at once. While he was putting them up again with a penitent show of extreme caution, Miss Arnays sat silent, softly passing the tips of her fingers over the bright braids of Clemency's hair.

" Now, Aunt Bessie, if you are arranging a little lecture for me, let Arthur come in for his share ; he is quite as bad as I am, though he does choose to look cross and philosophical. At this moment I know he would give his ears to be Colonel Edgecombe."

" No ; half my life," Arthur said, in an earnest tone of voice, which took both his hearers by surprise.

Miss Arnays looked anxiously at him. "Half your life to be talked of for three days! Oh, Arthur!"

"That was not what I meant," Arthur said, rather sullenly Clemency thought.

"No; let us keep to the question." she cried. "For real fame, for rightly deserved distinction, one might give up and do a great deal. I can't believe there is any harm in coveting it, or admiring those who have it."

Miss Arnays lowered her voice a little in replying. "How can ye honour me who seek honour one of another?" she said, softly. "That is the danger. It was over-valuing outside glory and honour that prevented men from knowing Him when He came; it often prevents us from knowing the best now; that is why I am sorry to see you both so easily dazzled and made envious by coming in contact with such a little glimmer of fame as this."

Clemency did not take her aunt's rebuke quite in such good part as usual. "What can make you think *I* am dazzled?" she said. "Well, we will not talk any more about it. Arthur shall play a game of backgammon with you, and I will give my whole mind to undoing the mistakes in your knitting you made while I was away last night."

CHAPTER V.

—— An English home—gray twilight pour'd
On dewy pastures, dewy trees,
Softer than sleep—all things in order stored,
A haunt of ancient Peace.

Tennyson.

On the high-road leading from Tunstall to Hemsley market, there was a certain gate from which, through a vista in the Combe Woods, a charming view of the whole of the little Combe Valley might be obtained. It was the stock picturesque sight of the neighbourhood; and when the families of the wealthy manufacturers of Tunstall and Hemsley had visitors, they brought them there in triumph, to show how little the beauty of the country was injured by factory chimneys and the smoke of furnace fires. The most captious were obliged to admit that, seen through its screen of woods, Combe presented as perfect a picture of rural beauty and quiet as could be found in any part of the island. The valley itself was a dip between two gently-sloping hills; at the bottom ran

a brisk little stream, fronted by the many-gabled old-
fashioned Combe Manor House ; beyond the river the
cottages of Thorpe Combe village climbed the further
hill, and were crowned by a low grey church at the top.

Mr. Serle's house was generally allowed to be the
most imposing feature of the scene. Spring, summer,
autumn, or winter, whether its red chimneys were
beautifully contrasted with the green leaves, flowers, or
fruit of the luxuriant creepers and vines that clasped
its old walls, or whether they only sent up their wreaths
of smoke against the sky, it had an aspect of ancient
peace about it, which seldom failed to inspire the spec-
tators with envy, and sometimes sent them away
wondering whether the petty discontents of life would
be felt as keenly under such a roof as elsewhere. If by
chance the loungers at the gate caught a glimpse of old
Mr. Serle setting off on his afternoon ride round his
farm, with a rosy grandchild seated on his sober cob
before him, and his pretty daughter Sydney walking by
his side ; or of George Serle, handsome and burly, stroll-
ing homewards across the yellow stubble-fields on a
September afternoon, with his gun over his shoulder ;
or of a gay group of children, headed by Aunt Siddie,
cowslipping on a spring morning in the low meadows
by the stream,—their estimation of the delights of a

country-life was sure to be raised ten-fold, and the Manor House probably remained ever afterwards their ideal abode of rural bliss, to be remembered and longed for in toilsome or weary hours.

It must be confesssed, however, that Combe Manor wore its best face to those who looked at it across the Combe Woods, and that a nearer inspection was apt to be a little disappointing. A very few days spent under the picturesque roof would have convinced the envious town's-folk that the outward aspect was very imperfectly reflected within. The Serle household was by no means a harmonious one, and of late years the causes of discord among its members had been growing daily more prominent. Old Mr. Serle himself was a gentle-tempered, easy-going, sociable man, and during many years of his life, while he had had a sensible active wife to guide his household and check his tendency to extravagance, he had been fairly prosperous and happy. His evil days began when he was left a widower, with a daughter hardly passed out of infancy, a son many years older, and a household all the more difficult to manage because it had never been clear to his mind, or to his neighbours', whether it ought to be regulated on a scale suitable to a country gentleman of one of the oldest families in the shire, or

to that of the farmer of the few acres which now alone
remained of all the large estate once owned by the
squires of Manor Combe. This uncertainty of aim had
a very unfortunate influence on the education and character of Mr. Serle's two children. They grew up un-
fitted for either position; neither cultivated enough
to adorn the one, nor sufficiently industrious and contented to be happy in the other. The son, many
degrees less gentlemanlike than his father, yet too
proud to bear the mortifications to which his deficien-
cies exposed him when he associated with people he had
been taught to consider his equals, fell into low company,
and caused his father so much anxiety, that when he at
length made a somewhat disadvantageous marriage, Mr.
Serle received the news quite thankfully, hoping that
new responsibilities would reclaim him from past follies.

Sydney was about twelve years old when her brother
George brought home his wife, a handsome showily
dressed personage, several years older than himself, and
of quite venerable antiquity, according to Sydney's
notions. In after years she often recalled the summer
afternoon of that arrival—how she and her father had
stood hand in hand at the house-door to receive the
bride and bridegroom, he with an anxious flush on his
cheek, the cause for which she had not comprehended

at the time, and she elated and happy at having a welcome to bestow; and how her sister-in-law's glance of ownership round the house as her husband complacently led her into it, dispelled her hospitable purposes, and taught her at once that she had lost her place in her old home for ever. She had been a little queen till that moment, bending father, brother, and servants to her caprices with an absolute but affectionate rule; that evening they all understood that they had fallen under a very different sway. Even old Mr. Serle's gentle graciousness of manner, which impressed most people with respect, did not preserve him from being extinguished, and thrust aside almost as ignominiously as his little daughter. Sydney never forgot how, when she went to wish her father good-night that evening, he held her longer than usual in his arms, and stroked her soft hair again and again with lingering pathetic fondness; she kissed him vehemently in return, and believed ever afterwards that the mutual caress sealed a compact between them, to stand by each other and resist the new tyranny that had come into the house. The alliance was not one calculated to promote peace in the family. Two weak, vehement, unreasonable, sensitive people, opposed to one coarse, strong-willed, sensible woman, were not likely to reap anything but suffering and constant irritation from their rebellion, and yet were nearly sure never to give in utterly and own themselves conquered.

Mrs. George Serle was not by any means an ill-intentioned person. She was coarse-minded, and not very scrupulous; but on the whole she meant to do her duty by her husband's family now that she had come among them. When she manœuvred to marry George Serle, she had expected to enter a much more prosperous household than Manor Combe proved to be, and consequently she felt justified in expressing loudly her disgust at the mismanagement which had produced such results, and in setting on foot a rigorous reformation. "It was for her children's good," she always said, when she encountered the obloquy sure to come upon economic reformers of every grade; and it must be confessed there was something respectable in the courage with which she carried out her unpopular measures. She had no conception of the torture which her practice of small irritating economies and disregard of little niceties and refinements in daily habits inflicted upon her father-in-law and Sydney. Still less could she understand the fatal estrangement which grew up between Mr. Serle and his son, when she instigated the latter to introduce improved methods of cultivation on the farm. The love with which Mr. Serle regarded every tangled briar hedge, and every gnarled tree that overshadowed and spoiled his corn-fields, was a sentiment that could not by any possibility enter into her practical mind. The old gentleman himself probably could not have given a comprehensible account of it. He did not know that the feelings of a poet or an artist lay unexpressed within him, and that when on dewy summer mornings he stood entranced on his door-step to admire the crimson heads of the poppies waving among his corn, and the great clumps of marsh marigolds burning like flakes of fire in his undrained meadows, he was seeing with eyes such as none of those round him were gifted with. Having no words to explain the thrill of delight these forms and colours gave him, he could only cherish each familiar object with silent jealous affection, and resent as a personal injury every attempt to change the aspects he had so long loved.

His son understood him as little as his daughter-in-law did; but he was too good-hearted not to suffer severely from the coldness and restraint between himself and his father, which his wife's interference had brought about. The two men, father and son, never disputed or complained of each other, but they cherished each towards the other a sore dull sense of injury, and of being

harshly judged, which embittered all their intercourse,
and left always an aching spot in their minds. The
father wondered always how the son to whom he had
forgiven so much could have the heart to take sides
against him; the son, seeing things pretty much
through his wife's eyes, wondered that his father should
have his children's interests so little at heart as to be
unable to give up his whims to further them. If Mrs.
George had been Até herself, and had brought the
apple of discord into the Manor House with her, she
could not have divided the family more completely.
Of late years, the contest between the two parties had
been rather less unequal than formerly, for Mrs. George
had begun to find Sydney a formidable rival. Not
that Sydney ever troubled herself about the farm
management or the household business. Mrs. George
had some reason to complain of her, that she never did
a useful hand's turn from the time she rose till she
went to bed, but, spite of that, she began to exercise
an influence in the house, which rendered her presence
there gall to her sister-in-law. Not only did she
monopolise the entire attention of the few visitors who
came to the Manor, causing them, Mrs. George complained, to pay no more regard to her than if she were
a chair or a table, but she encouraged her brother to

come to her for sympathy whenever there had been a conjugal dispute, and had even inspired him with courage once or twice of late to follow her advice instead of his wife's. What was still more unbearable, the very children turned traitors, and openly preferred pretty Aunt Siddie's useless smiles and fitful favours, to the steady washings, scoldings, physickings, and general settings to rights which their own mother wore herself out in bestowing upon them.

Even a more generous tempered person than Mrs. George might not have liked such a universally favoured rival always in her way, and to her practical mind it had daily been growing clearer that the same roof could not much longer peaceably shelter them both. Having no intention of taking herself and her belongings from pleasant Manor Combe, and knowing that old Mr. Serle would certainly never permit his daughter to leave his house except for a home of her own, her hopes were fixed on the chance of Sydney's marrying early, and most of the schemes on which she had exercised her ingenuity of late had the promotion of that desirable object for their end. She took no pains to conceal either wishes or schemes from any one. She did not consider that any one would blame her, who had daughters of her own growing up, for taking some

pains to get her pretty sister-in-law married out of the
way; and she believed that Sydney's indignation at her
plain speaking was nothing but an air—one of the
ridiculous Serle airs—which she was quite resolved to
put down in her own daughters with a high hand, if
they should ever show an inclination to wear them.

In the long dark afternoons of this winter, when Mrs.
George settled herself early to her needlework in the
one parlour that had a fire in it, and the cold was too
severe to permit of escape to the damp unused drawing-
room or the draughty hall, Sydney's temper was tried
by many an hour's advice, and many a lecture on her
folly in always bestowing her smiles and favours on
the least eligible of her admirers, to the neglect of the
serious minded among them, whom Mrs. George favoured. Sydney's spirit would supply her with sharp
retorts for the first quarter of an hour. She was vehement, and a great deal cleverer than Mrs. George; in a
short word-fight she might have held her own, but she
was no match in persistence; she could not go on saying the same stupid provoking things over and over
again, a dozen times in an hour, and she could never
for long keep the tears out of her eyes, or prevent her
voice from being choked with sobs. After a short
struggle she was sure to break down ignominiously in

tears, and then the avalanche of words fell down on her head uninterruptedly, and she had just to sit still and bear it. Sometimes old Mr. Serle would wake up from his afternoon nap while talk of this kind was going on; and the dismayed expression of his gentle face at the sight of tears in Sydney's pretty eyes, brought something like compunction even to Mrs. George's obtuse conscience.

He never inquired the cause of the dispute, or attempted to put in a word. It always puzzled him how women could choose to make grievances worse by talking about them ; but by-and-by he would miss his snuff-box or his spectacles, and calling Sydney to help him to look for them, would take an opportunity of stroking her hair unperceived, or whispering her pet name, and Sydney would crouch down by his side, and rest her soft cheek against his knee and be happy, till Mrs. George's disgust was aroused, and she exploded again in a contemptuous tirade against idleness, and sentiment that all ended in talk, under which father and daughter winced equally.

A stormy afternoon was almost sure to follow one of Sydney's visits to High Combe ; for as Mrs. George considered Mrs. Edgecombe's injudicious patronage the main source of Sydney's false estimate of her own importance, she always felt it incumbent on her to

administer a stringent course of snubbing as an
antidote to such undue elevation. On the day after
Sydney's drive to Hemsley, when she had not only
received a birthday present, but had witnessed Colonel
Edgecombe's return home, Mrs. George hardly knew how
to make the snubbing severe enough to equal the occasion. She had, moreover, one or two private grievances to
complain of, which with some ingenuity might be fixed
on Sydney. Mrs. Edgecombe had declined entering
the house, though she had prepared luncheon for her.
If Sydney's influence were as great as she pretended, she
surely might have used it to prevent her sister's hospitality from being slighted. What was worse, Sydney had
neglected to deliver a certain note at a house at Hemsley, which Mrs. George had prepared expressly that her
correspondent might be edified by the sight of Sydney
driving up to his door in Mrs. Edgecombe's carriage.
It was a note of invitation, too, and it was addressed to
one of Sydney's supposed admirers, a certain grave
middle-aged surgeon at Hemsley, whose pretentions
Mrs. George was most determined to favour. She had
taken some trouble to prepare an entertainment for
him on the ensuing Sunday, and she really hardly
knew how to say enough about Sydney's ingratitude
in making her forethought of no avail.

It was a dim grey afternoon, slight showers of snow every now and then falling, which drove every one early into the house, and Sydney had to sit for three long hours plying her needle, and listening to her sister's lecture. She did not attempt to answer that day, neither did any tears come ; on the contrary, to Mrs. George's intense provocation, little dreamy smiles played round the corners of her mouth. Her sister-in-law's words blew over her like idle wind. Something of the excitement of yesterday hung about her still, and lifted her a little above the level of her every-day annoyances. She could look over them for a few hours, and bask in the reflected light of another person's great joy. She had never before been brought into contact with such deep feeling as she had seen on the faces of the two who had met yesterday, and it had greatly moved her, waking quite unwonted thoughts in her usually self-occupied mind. She had perhaps never before in her life forgotten herself for so long together. It was not till the long afternoon was over that her thoughts were forced back into their usual groove by a remark which her sister-in-law shot after her as she was mounting the stairs to her own room.

"It was just nonsense," Mrs. George declared, " for Sydney to pretend to rejoice over Colonel Edgecombe's

return home. She would be in a different mood by-
and-by when she had found out how completely it
would banish her from High Combe. Her godmother
would have no thoughts to spare for her now that she
had her son, and the house would always be full of
fine visitors, for whom she would not be considered fit
company."

Sydney walked straight on without turning her head,
but this prophecy did not fall as lightly on her ear as the
previous discourse had done. When she reached her own
room, she put her candle down on the table, opened the
low window in the roof and leaned out, looking towards
the High Combe Woods with a very forlorn dreary
feeling in her poor little heart. She could not see any
part of the house, it was hidden among the trees; but
the spire of Combe Church rose above them, and she
fancied she could still descry the folds of the great
flag which the villagers had run up as soon as their
Squire's arrival had been made known among them.
A dozen times that day she had looked from her window
at the flag with a sort of triumph, as if it had something
to do with her, because she had known of the joyous
event it celebrated before most other people. It was
hard to be convinced, not only that she was to have
no share in the joy, but that she was to be made less

happy by it. She folded her arms on the window-sill and leaned on them for a long time revolving the dreary thought in her mind. It was a windless evening, and the air was only frosty enough to cool her flushed cheek pleasantly. The snow had ceased to fall, and through a rift in the snow-clouds the full moon looked out just then, showing all the beautiful sights that were to be seen from Sydney's garret-window: the snow-powdered trees sloping up the hill, till they touched the sky ; the red glow of the Tunstall furnace-fires flushing and fading on the opposite horizon; the still, solitary fields near, so pure in their winter robes ; the moving lights among the farm buildings, which showed that the business of the day was not yet drawn to a close. Sydney looked at all this beauty with preoccupied eyes. She had seen it on a hundred evenings, and it had no particular power to soothe or charm her. It was just Vale Combe Manor Farm where she had lived all her life, and where just now a great many things were happening to annoy her.

The mental pictures her fancy called up were far more really present with her than the actual objects on which her eyes fell. Visions of the well-known rooms at High Combe filled with strange faces, and of herself, somehow or other, looking on at festivities in

which she had no share ; of Mrs. Edgecombe, with her
son on one side, and Clemency Franklyn on the other,
passing her in Hemsley Market, and being too busy
talking and laughing together to notice her. Her
foolish heart quite swelled with self-pity at the thought,
and with resolute hopelessness she went on conjuring
up fancied scenes from her own future, all in harmony
with her dreary mood. The house in Hemsley Market
where her sister was so anxious to see her established
as mistress, rose before her eyes, looking duller and
uglier than she had ever thought it before.

Towards that goal the strong will of her sister was
drifting her, and she felt just then as if the chances of
her being able to withstand the current were hardly
worth reckoning. Only yesterday, when she had driven
past the house, she had felt a little glow of satisfaction
on observing that Mr. Humphreys furtively from the
surgery window, and his mother and sisters openly
from the upper rooms, were watching her with admiring eyes as she drove down the street. Now the
recollection of this tribute to her consequence only
added to her dismay. If all those people wanted to
have her there, how was she to stand out against them ?
That grave, self-possessed man, who used such long
words in talking of little Willie's ailments that even

her father was overawed ; the active, bustling mother ;
the two tall, talkative sisters, in whose presence Sydney
always felt herself so very small and extinguished,—all
these drawing or pushing her one way ; and to oppose
them she found not even a very strong resolution or
decided wish, only a weary sinking in her own heart,
and an acknowledgment of her powerlessness to struggle.
If Mrs. Edgecombe ceased to care for her and uphold
her, there would be no further use in struggling.

Then Sydney drooped her head on her crossed arms,
and wished, oh! so vehemently, that there was some one
in the world both strong and kind, who cared enough
for her to stand up for her, and not let her poor little
weak will be always crushed down. For it was not true
meekness that made her yielding, it was simple incapa-
city for carrying out her own will ; while she longed
all the time for a little taste of freedom, as only undis-
ciplined people who chance to be both wilful and weak
can long.

If the air had been as full of mischief seeds as it
was half-an-hour before of wandering snow-flakes, and
if Sydney had opened a door in her heart for them
to enter, as wide as she did her window, she would
hardly have prepared herself for future temptation
more disastrously than by indulging the discontented

self-pitying fancies of that one idle hour. She was roused at last by one of the children coming to tell her that they were all sitting down to tea without her. Absence from meals was considered a serious offence at Manor Combe, but Sydney lingered to wash the traces of tears from her face, change her dress, and fasten round her throat the slender gold chain and jewelled locket which Mrs. Edgecombe had given her the day before.

Her father liked her to wear pretty things, and her sister-in-law did not, for which reasons Sydney never neglected an opportunity of displaying such as she possessed. That night she pulled out her long curls, and arranged her draperies with extra care, yet with a little trepidation. She knew that Mrs. George would consider her careful toilette and display of Mrs. Edgecombe's present, after the lecture she had been giving her, an act of defiance ; and she could neither make up her mind to forego it, nor accomplish it without many tremblings.

She had never looked prettier in her life than she did when she opened the door of the parlour where the whole family were assembled round the tea-table. Her large, very well-opened brown eyes glistened even more brightly than usual through a lingering mist of tears ; her cheeks had a shade of richer colour, and she held her pretty little head high in the air with a half-defiant, half-frightened gesture, that would have said a great deal to any one at all initiated into the family politics.

Spite of her struggle to be brave, it was a relief to discover that an unusual buzz of conversation pervaded the room, and that a strange voice mixed with it. Her sister-in-law was seated at the head of the table, very crestfallen (Sydney perceived at the first glance), and extremely conscious of the morning gown and untidy cap she was still wearing. Her father and brother had risen from their places and were standing by the fire; between them, his towering head almost touching the ceiling of the low room, was Colonel Edgecombe.

Sydney had only seen him for a minute the evening before, but she knew him again in an instant, and felt her heart stand still with surprise, and then beat quick and high with pleasure and triumph. It was extremely silly, she told herself afterwards, to be so glad, but there was no use in denying that the foolish, fluttering joy had been there. It was such a contrast to all she had been picturing to herself. She felt suddenly lifted miles away from the fear of Mrs. George's displeasure, that had made her hand tremble as she opened the door, and from all the vexations of the afternoon, up into a different world, where ill-natured triumph could not for the time find room to enter. When she had answered Colonel Edgecombe's cordial greeting, she took her place at the tea-table and busied herself unobtrusively in quieting the children's clamours for their tea, and in covering, as far as lay in her power, Mrs. George's sulky discomfiture. She had no wish to join in the conversation that went on briskly between her father and their guest, but she felt injured whenever the children's chatter, or her sister-in-law's noisy movements with the tea equipage, caused her to lose a word. Not that any new or interesting topic was started—it was all very common-place talk, such as she might have heard any evening in the year.

Colonel Edgecombe told them how he had followed a new path in the plantation to see where it led, and had found himself unexpectedly close to the gate of Combe Manor House; and from the mention of the new wood-path, Mr. Serle had been led to dilate on his present favourite grievance—a right of way through one of his fields which the opening out of the new road through the Combe Woods had incited the Tunstall people to claim. Sydney had heard her father tell the history of this dispute in precisely the same words fifty times before, and she was used to the signs of indifference or weariness with which it was usually received by his auditors. She had learned to dread his beginning upon it, and to long for the concluding sentence ; to-night she wished it had been twice as long. It was so pleasant to look up now and then, and see that Colonel Edgecombe's head was still bent down deferentially to listen, and that the same eager, interested expression was on his face. He clearly did not find her father's conversation so very wearying. Sydney promised herself that she would never be vexed again when Mrs. George's rude brothers yawned or interrupted her father a dozen times in the course of a narration.

"Yes, you are quite right," Colonel Edgecombe said, when the story came to an end at last. "I expect, when I have seen more of the country, I shall not know how to be grateful enough to you for keeping one spot safe from change. I have been fretting over improvements all day. No one who has not been absent from England ten years would believe how happy I felt when I found myself facing your orchard wall, and discovered that the coping-stone George and I pulled off the corner fourteen years ago, lay on the ground still, and had never been replaced. How deliciously like itself this room looks. Miss Serle, is not that the very same oak chest I used to perch you upon when George and I were getting our fishing-tackle ready, and you would persist in spoiling my flies? Do you remember?" Colonel Edgecombe had moved up the room while he was speaking, and now stood close behind Sydney's chair.

She had to look up to answer, but the reference to old times had dispelled her shyness.

"Indeed I do remember many times when I stood there till I was tired, and thought you very cruel for putting me up. But there is one day I recollect more distinctly than all the rest. Clemency Franklyn was spending the day with me. She would turn all the worms out of your bait-box into the garden, because, she said, she could not bear to think of your putting hooks through them, and you were really very angry when you found it out. You frightened us both terribly."

"And you have treasured the recollection against me all these years; but that is too bad. I don't believe I really was angry. I think it far more likely that it was you and Miss Franklyn who terribly frightened me. The chest looks a very comfortable place to be perched upon. I give any one leave to put me up there who likes."

The last sentence was addressed to two of the

children, on whose curly heads Colonel Edgecombe had placed his large hands so as gently to turn up their faces towards his.

" Now, which of you will put me up ? "

They stared, half frightened at the dark bearded face bent over them, till the eldest found courage to answer solemnly,

" You are too big. Your head would go right through the ceiling."

Then Aunt Siddie's gravity gave way before the exquisitely ludicrous idea of Colonel Edgecombe sitting on their sideboard with his head through the ceiling ; and there was a general laugh.

" Ah, you don't know how small I have had to make myself, sometimes," Colonel Edgecombe went on, quite gravely. " I look big to-day because I have just come home, and every one is glad to see me ; but by-and-bye it will be different. I shall shrink to my proper size, and be able to sit on the shelf very comfortably. It is what I have come home to do, and my mother and Miss Franklyn have been encouraging me to do it contentedly."

A puzzled look on Sydney's face and a little contemptuous sniff from Mrs. George here reminded Colonel Edgecombe that his present auditors were probably not people with whom it was safe to talk nonsense. They might fancy he was making a joke of *them.* To remove the impression (he never could bear the thought of leaving anything but a pleasant impression behind him from whatever company he came out) he drew one of the children's chairs to the table, asked Mrs. George's permission to sit down, and settled himself for such an easy chat as every one, the children included, could enter into. Even Mrs. George's ill-humour yielded to the pleasure of being appealed to for information concerning old friends who lived in her part of the country; and George Serle's spirits were raised by recollections of bygone holiday sports to a higher pitch than they had reached since Mrs. George had taken upon herself the task of keeping them in order. It was many a day since such pleasant laughter had been heard in the Combe sitting-room, or such an agreeable common interest had drawn the divided family together. Before long the children found courage to gather round Colonel Edgecombe's chair, and clamour for stories about tiger hunts; and then by degrees it oozed out that Aunt Siddie had been in the habit of telling them tales in the twilight, all about India, and about a brave man who had driven hundreds of wicked black men into a river, and helped to gain a great victory.

"It was you—you are the brave man. Now, is he not, Aunt Siddie?" they persisted, mercilessly.

Aunt Siddie thought her cheeks would never leave off burning, especially as Colonel Edgecombe remained silent for a moment, with a thoughtful look on his face, quietly stroking the long hair of the little girl who had been most eager in identifying him with Aunt Siddie's hero. Could he be angry with her, Sydney wondered. He looked up suddenly. Their eyes met, and he smiled, just such a radiant smile, softening and brightening brow, eye, and lip, as transformed Mrs. Edgecombe's proud face now and then, and made it loveable in Sydney's eyes.

"Shall I tell you what I am thinking?" he asked, quickly. "That you must not let me hear more of these stories, or I shall find myself really growing too big for the shelf. Yes; I am quite in earnest. To be talked about at home, in the houses one is always picturing to one's self, is the only kind of fame one really cares for. I have not done anything yet to deserve that the children should hear stories about me; but if I ever do, I shall care more to think of such being told here than for all the newspaper trumpetings in the world."

Sydney did not quite understand the thought, but the

feeling revealed in look and tone could not escape her. When Colonel Edgecombe had taken his departure it was not unnatural that she should relieve the monotony of her evening's work by pondering a good deal over these last words of his to her. She did not know how much his pleasure in the cordiality of his welcome home was enhanced by recollections of the sorrows and mortifications he had had to endure there in past times. Not having the same understanding of his history that Clemency had, the strength of his home feelings surprised and interested her ; and her unoccupied imagination wove never-ending webs of fancy round him.

CHAPTER VI.

O the little more, and how much it is !
  And the little less, and what worlds away !   :
How a sound shall quicken content to bliss,
  Or a breath suspend the blood's best play,
And life be a proof of this.

Browning.

THE interest excited by Colonel Edgecombe's return
was great and lasting enough to satisfy even his mother's
estimate of his importance.   It was long since the Tunstall people had had any one among them with so much
claim to be considered a hero, and they were determined
to show that they estimated the advantage to its full
extent.   Even if there had been no story about him,
his gay sociable temper and cordial manner to rich and
poor would have made him a great gain to any country
society.   As it was, there was scarcely a person in the
neighbourhood who did not find his or her life more or
less brightened by his presence that winter.   The
county magnates exchanged unwonted entertainments
in his honour, and the humble townsfolk enjoyed the

almost daily pleasure of seeing him ride down Tunstall High Street, and of conjecturing concerning the business or pleasure that brought him so often into their little town. It seemed to one or two people even as if the season itself shared the general hilarity, and allowed a certain premature air of spring to soften the rigour of the early months of the year. Certainly the young ladies' winter bonnets made unusual haste to exchange their dark trimmings for more becoming colours. People began to find out earlier than usual that the lengthening days were favourable for country rambles, and picnics were planned to the Combe woods before the bulrushes flowered in Mr. Serle's fields, or the catkins hung out their golden balls in the High Combe hedges. Of course there were a few dissentients from the general good humour, who chose to make a grievance of their neighbours being merry without sufficient cause.

Arthur Yonge was one of the most determined of the grumblers. He and Clemency Franklyn seldom met without quarrelling over their different opinions respecting the little gaieties and pleasure schemes with which the mind of Tunstall was rife that spring. It was not that Arthur might not have had his full share in them if he had chosen. Colonel Edgecombe and Clemency Franklyn were equally set upon drawing him into the society they frequented, and their united influence would have effected any revolution in Tunstall opinion at that time.

Colonel Edgecombe sought Arthur's society from a Hamon-like desire to win over the only person, with whom he had come in contact, who was not disposed to court him; and Clemency persisted in pressing invitations upon him, because she wanted the countenance of her old companion and monitor to silence some scruples that troubled her sometimes, as to the frivolity of her present pursuits.

They courted and insisted in vain. Arthur grew more sulkily independent than ever, and resented their efforts at patronage (as he called them) so fiercely that Miss Arnays felt moved now and then, when he was sitting alone with her, to remonstrate on the unchristian spirit of pride she feared he was fostering. She could not understand why anyone should be averse to receiving kindnesses, she to whom joyful giving and thankful receiving were equally natural—the very breath of her life. It puzzled her, too, that her gentle assurances of Colonel Edgecombe's good will and kind intentions invariably had the effect of increasing instead of mollifying Arthur's ill-humour. Miss Arnays had many opportunities of inflicting her gentle little lectures; for Arthur seldom failed to come and sit with her in the evenings when Clemency was away at High Combe, or visiting at other houses with her High Combe friends. He seemed scrupulously anxious that Aunt Bessie should never have a solitary evening, yet his efforts at companionship were limited to sitting opposite to her for two or three hours at a time, tormenting the contents of her work-basket and grumbling over scraps of gossip about Combe doings, which he yet would bring upon himself by pertinacious cross-questioning.

He showed a perverse ingenuity in extracting subjects of offence from the most harmless sayings, and even when Aunt Bessie reduced herself to absolute silence, his serenity was not secured. There was scarcely an object on which his eye fell, which did not irritate him, from the heads of the opposite neighbours peering over their blinds to watch the Edgecombe's carriage coming down the street, to the great bouquets of spring flowers which now always filled Aunt Bessie's purple vases. He even quarrelled with the west wind and the soft February showers for tempting the High Combe flowers to bloom so unseasonably, and disgusted Clemency by protesting that the scent of early violets made him ill. It was hard on Aunt

Bessie that the worst exhibitions of this captious humour were reserved for her solitary evenings. Arthur had lucid intervals, but these always occurred at the rare times when on coming in he found Clemency alone with her aunt, and occupied with some one of the quiet studies they had pursued diligently together, before more exciting amusements had thrust them into the background. On such occasions, he felt as if he had suddenly wakened from a nightmare dream, and the sense of escape from its oppression made him quite foolishly light-hearted and glad.

Every object in the little room and the two kind faces of his friends seemed to grow brighter, fairer, and a thousand times dearer than he had ever known them to be before. Life seemed to open out brightly and richly before him, holding out all its best prizes ready to his hand ; the most difficult tasks seemed easy, the most wearisome labour delightful, and he could not but take his two friends into the confidence of his happy mood. Miss Arnays used to fix her grave eyes on his eager face, with a look of mournful wonder that would have been dispiriting if Clemency had not accepted his brilliant prophecies, with an entire and easy belief that made him independent of other sympathy. As he watched the answering light of enthusiasm in her face, he wondered

how he could ever have been so silly as to let anything
trouble him, so faithless as to doubt the kindness of his
two friends, who, sitting there in the old places, with
everything around them the same, could not surely have
changed towards him in their hearts. Of all the pain
he had been feeling lately there remained only, quite
down at the bottom of his mind, a secret dread of the
passing away of the hour, and the mood it had brought·

As the evening wore on, the striking of the hours
and half-hours began to startle him with a little
sting of pain. The eager flow of talk abated gradually, and for the last half-hour or so he would
sit silent, watching the hands of the clock creeping
on towards the time at which it was his custom to
take leave, and wishing dreamily that he had the
power to arrest them in their course for an indefinite
period, beyond which he need not look. He did not
want his companions to move, or speak to him. He
would have been content if he and they could have
remained for ever with the present spell of calm
dreamy content resting on them—Aunt Bessie, leaning
back in her chair, with closed eyes, and lips gently
moving, as she murmured softly to herself the words of
some favourite hymn or passage of Scripture, according to her wont in moments of abstraction ; Clemency,

on a stool at her feet, her face a little turned away, her drooping eye-lashes softening eyes that had been radiant with mirth all the evening, her hands busied with her work, or lazily turning the leaves of some book they had been reading and discussing together; and he at liberty to look from one to the other, or let his eye wander among the tokens of daily occupation that filled the room, pleasing himself with the thought that each one of them was connected with some trifling event in which he had taken part, and that they never could have the same interest to anyone else in the world that they had to him. When at last the clock struck ten, and Aunt Bessie started from her reverie, and Clemency looked up with a remark on their preoccupation, it did not always at once occur to him, that while his thoughts had never wandered away from them, he had probably had very little place in theirs. The uncomfortable reflection waited to make itself heard till the friendly good nights had died away on his ear, and the gloomy silence of his own dark home had swallowed him up.

Clemency did not wish to be unkind or fickle in her behaviour towards an old friend. She had made very eager efforts to draw him into sharing the new interests and amusements that had opened out to her that spring, and when he persisted in keeping aloof, she could not help being provoked at the perverseness which made him choose that particular time to be unusually cross in. Why could he not be as happy as everyone else in the world seemed just then? The very airs of heaven were breathing more kindly than usual; the fields and trees clothing themselves in brighter colours, and the sunshine flooding the earth with a happier radiance than had glorified any former spring-time. She had no particular reason for being unusually happy, except the fine weather, and the high spirits of her neighbours,—why could not Arthur Yonge enjoy it all as much as she did?

The only drawback to her perfect content was a certain anxious, slightly disapproving, expression, which she had once or twice detected on Aunt Bessie's face, when she was trying to make her understand how it was that her love for Tunstall scenery, and delight in everything connected with the neighbourhood, had increased so rapidly since the beginning of the year. It was embarrassing to be reminded of former disparaging remarks, and longings for change. She could generally satisfy herself by saying that her aunt's constant admonitions had at last brought her to a more easily satisfied state of mind; but once or twice, when she realised how very disagreeable the thought of any change taking place in her life had become to her, she felt a little frightened herself. She had hitherto lived in the present, brightly and contentedly enough, but it had not looked very real to her : it was but a passage to some unknown future, which hung before her like a golden mist, into which her eyes were never weary of peering. Now the future seemed to have moved away into a very dim distance, it could wait till she had leisure to think of it again ; the immediate time—yesterday, to-day, and to-morrow—brought so many things to remember or expect, and their events were so distinct and real, that she had no inclination to look further away. Aunt Bessie had often advised her to live from day to day, and now at last she was doing it. Not consciously at first, however. She did not begin to examine her own state of mind, or make excuses for her unwonted happiness, till the first glow of her content had a little faded away.

It was the interruption of a week of rainy weather, coming at the end of the bright spring, that forced an unwelcome fit of self-inspection upon her. On the first morning when she was wakened by the patter of rain against her windows, she did not think her grief at the break-up of the fine weather at all exaggerated. It had been so pleasant while it

lasted. She could not help thinking sorrowfully that
the first freshness of early summer would have passed
away before there could be any more rides among the
lanes or rambles through the Combe Woods for her.
The battered state of the azaleas and rhododendrons
that Colonel Edgecombe had transplanted from Combe
to their little garden, in the beginning of the spring,
and watered himself so diligently ever since they showed
promise of flowering, made her quite melancholy. She
mourned over the destruction of their beautiful
blossoms, and pitied their forlorn looks, as if they had
been people who had met with a sudden downfall of
fortune. No one would ever take the trouble of water-
ing them again, and yet how lovely they had been a
few hours before. For one day Clemency forgave herself
for sitting listlessly over her books and her drawing,
and for wandering to the window every now and then,
to lament over the devastation the wind and rain were
making ; but when another and another rainy day
found her restless and unable to enter thoroughly into
her old pursuits, and when she perceived that her
aunt's eyes often rested anxiously on her, she began to
take herself seriously to task.

"I see how it is, Aunt Bessie," she said, one afternoon, when she had changed her employment three

times, and her aunt had sighed audibly over each change. " You think I am thoroughly spoiled by all the visiting and excitement I have had lately. You are just now despairing of me in your heart, and wondering what I shall be when I go to live at the Red House, since I am so soon upset by a few unusual pleasures."

"My dear, I have been young myself," Aunt Bessie said, quietly, " and very foolish too. It would be harsh, indeed if I were to despair of you at the first symptom of over-love of pleasure I have seen."

" Aunt Bessie, now listen to me. I am going to leave my drawing, and you must not sigh ; it is not that I am tired of it, but that I want to come and sit on your footstool and talk to you. I really have some-thing to say."

Clemency settled herself in her favourite posture for idle moments ; but the proposed communication did not come at once ; there was a long silence.

" Aunt Bessie," she began at last, " what I want to say is, that I love you better than any one else in the whole world, a thousand times better. I begin to think that I don't really like any one but you."

" And that is why rainy days, when you and I are left alone to enjoy each other's sole company, are so difficult to get over," Aunt Bessie answered, smiling.

"I think it *is* the reason why I have been so unsettled and felt so dissatisfied all this week. I have been comparing other people with you, and thinking how much better you are than any one else; and how much —yes, how very much more, after all, you care for me."

"Of course I care more for you than any one else can; but I don't see why that should make you restless. Have you not known it all your life?"

"Yes, indeed. 'And what I want to tell you is, that I love you best, and that I am so glad I am quite sure I do. Aunt Bessie, I will tell you something. I find I have been trying an experiment. You know you have often said to me that the highest thing is to live wholly in other people's lives, and have nothing of one's own. I have been doing that lately, and it was very pleasant while it lasted. Only for *that*, things should go on always the same; it does not do to have a break, and then to discover that the other people's lives can go on quite as well without one. Your life could not go on as well without me; that is the reason I love you, and——"

"My dear, I don't think you understand what I mean, by living in other people's lives."

"Yes, I do. I used not. I used always to keep a beautiful little corner quite to myself to dream in. Lately I have not been thinking of myself at all. I have not wanted to build one castle in the air. I was growing as contented and as disposed to think well of every one, Mrs. Franklyn included, as you are. Now the rain has come and washed all my goodness out of me. I feel as cross as Arthur Yonge on his worst days. Last night, when I was grumbling about the weather, he actually looked at me as if he pitied me, and understood what I felt. I was so provoked; more angry than I have ever been with any one since I was a child. I think it is very absurd of *him* to come here through the rain when no one else ever does."

"No one else—but Mrs. Franklyn and one of the dear little children from the Red House called yesterday, and several poor people have been here whose wants we have been able to relieve. The rainy days have not been empty of interest, dear. We have had opportunities of doing one or two neighbourly things."

"Aunt Bessie, how good you are, and how bad I must be. I forgot all about the poor people. The days have seemed empty of interest to me. I am not patient and unselfish like you."

"You are young, dear."

"When you say 'You are young,' and look down on me with that far-away look in your eyes, Aunt Bessie, you half-frighten me. It seems as if to be young meant something very sad to you."

"No, dear, not sad; it only means that since you still have all your lessons to learn, it would be very unreasonable to expect you to know them now."

"These rainy days have taught me one lesson: to make a great deal of you and stay at home more than I have done lately. They have not missed me at Combe all this week—not so much as once. The alterations in the conservatory have been going on all the same, I dare say; and they will have finished arranging the pictures and the Indian curiosities that I helped to unpack. They will not have waited for me to go on with anything."

"Most likely not. It would have been a pity to wait for you. You know you are going to the Red House on Saturday to stay there till after that evening party is over, about which your mother is now so busy. As you are going there on purpose to help your mother, I shall tell Mrs. Edgecombe that she must not send over for you three or four times a-week, as she has done lately. It would not do."

"Oh, dear! And when I come back the best part of

the summer will be over. It will be too late to ride in the afternoons, and all the dog-roses and honeysuckles will have faded in the hedges. Colonel Edgecombe showed me a tree so full of pink buds, the last time we rode down the lane behind Vale Combe Manor, and we planned to go and gather the roses when they were nearly blown."

"There are plenty of briar hedges near the Red House, and the dear little children will help you to gather the roses."

"I dare say they will. Well, I am going to begin to be cheerful. Arthur Yonge shall not pity me again to-night. Lie back in your chair and rest, Aunt Bessie. I will take your knitting to the window, and you will be surprised when you open your eyes to see how it has grown."

Aunt Bessie was not destined to have that surprise, however. Before she had quite composed herself for her afternoon sleep the sound of carriage-wheels roused her, and the next minute Mrs. Edgecombe and her son entered the room together. They had been of late very constant visitors. Colonel Edgecombe was now almost as much at home in the little sitting-room as Arthur Yonge, and Miss Arnays had grown so accustomed to his sauntering in and out at uncertain times, that she

allowed herself to be as little interrupted by his coming
and going as by Arthur's. To-day she was disposed
to take a more active part than usual in the entertainment of her visitors. It had occurred to her during
the few minutes while she lay back with her eyes shut,
that perhaps she had too often lately allowed her
thoughts to be absorbed by her own favourite subjects
of contemplation.

Difficulties might be rising up in the bright young
lives over which she had long watched, and she might
be failing to understand them for want of vigilance.
Her sharpened observation led her to detect an unusual
expression in the countenances of her visitors, but it
was not at all what she had expected to see. For the
first time for many weeks there was a slight cloud on Mrs.
Edgecombe's face, and it was reflected a little more
decidedly on her son's. They both talked and laughed,
and tried hard to be unconstrained; but, when they
addressed each other, there was a certain measured
accent in their tones, and a careful weighing of words,
which, between close friends, shows a more perilous
state of mutual annoyance than direct accusation or
actual petulance. Mrs. Edgecombe talked the most
and the fastest; Colonel Edgecombe roamed restlessly
about the room, now striking a note on Clemency's

piano, now putting a touch into her drawing, now taking the faded flowers in and out of the purple vases. He did not look exactly angry, but there was a certain down-drawing of the corners of his mouth, half-obstinate, half-petulant, which recalled old Mr. Edgecombe's face in his least amiable moods more vividly than Aunt Bessie liked to remember it. Clemency asked an unimportant question about the occupations in which they had all lately been engaged at Combe, and a sudden deepening of Mrs. Edgecombe's colour showed that she had touched on a vexed question.

"Oh, no! We have done nothing. I have been perfectly idle all the week. Walter does not consider that in-door employments are suitable for rainy days. He is like that naughty boy in 'Struwwelpeter,' who said, ' When it pours it is nicest out-of-doors.' He has ridden or walked over every ploughed field in Combe, High and Low, since the rain began ; and I have sat at the window counting the rain-drops."

" I have had engagements on business every day this week," Colonel Edgecombe answered, shortly. " There has been nothing in the weather to prevent my keeping them. Surely, mother, you are not so unreasonable as to expect me to stay in-doors all day whenever it rains ? " .

"Since you stayed in-doors nearly all day while it was fine perhaps I might expect it. Of course I don't care in the least how often you go out, or when; only since you never before, in spite of all my entreaties, gave one single hour to business, I was not prepared for such sudden absorbing devotion to it. Unreason will always be a common complaint at Combe, I fear."

Here Aunt Bessie broke in with an utterly irrelevant remark, on the difficulty of purchasing good tea at Tunstall, and Colonel Edgecombe threw himself down on Clemency's music-stool and executed a thundering scale up and down the keys. When he had finished he twisted the stool so as to face Clemency, who had kept her seat by the window, and, bending over towards her, addressed her in a low tone.

"Can you understand this? I can't tell you how it pains me. There is only you I can trust to make it right between us; you know her better than I do. I should never have got wrong if you had stayed at Combe. You always please her."

Clemency wondered afterwards why these words and the tone in which they were spoken sent such a warm thrill of happiness to her heart, and why she could hardly keep her voice from trembling as she answered—

"Oh, no; not always. I have vexed her sometimes.

I know quite well how unhappy you must be now. The comfort is that she is so generous. She will hardly know how to forgive herself when she sees, as she will soon, that there has been no intended neglect or wrong on your part."

"Thank you for saying that. If I only could understand at what part of my conduct she feels aggrieved; but I am quite in the dark. She is not really angry at my leaving her so much alone. I never knew her exacting in that way."

"Nor I; it would be quite unlike her to grudge your spending your time in any way you liked."

"Besides, I have not been absent for my own pleasure, or on business that concerned myself. I have been hard at work on old Mr. Serle's account. He is in trouble, as I fancy he has often been before. His son and daughter-in-law want him to part with some of his land to raise money to pay a troublesome debt. He appealed to me almost heart-broken; and I have been doing my best to see that the poor old man's will was not harshly overborne. I should have thought my mother would have sympathised in such a case."

"So she would, if only —— "

"Pray go on, it is so necessary that I should understand."

"I hardly like to say it. I hope so earnestly I am mistaken. But I am afraid I have noticed lately that she is rather prejudiced against all the Serles."

Colonel Edgecombe's brow darkened. "I hope, indeed, that you are mistaken. I should be sorry to think her capable of taking prejudices against old neighbours, and of quarrelling with me for not sharing them. I don't see how there is to be any peace if that is possible. I wish to defer to her wishes and judgment in everything; she has been supreme here hitherto, and I am sure I have no wish to interfere; but if she behaves capriciously, and expects me to behave capriciously, to old friends, I don't know what I shall do."

"I did not mean to accuse her of caprice. I am sure she will always really wish you to do what you yourself think right to everybody. She may be vexed sometimes to find that you and she don't think alike about people; but she will be happier, and have most rest in the end, for finding that you keep consistently to your own opinion."

"Of course I must keep to my own opinion. Thank you for the hope that rest and peace will come to us in the end, in spite of a few differences. No two people I suppose can quite manage without them; it is ridiculous of us to be made so unhappy by a simple difference of opinion; but there has been so much gloom and discord in our house in past times, that the faintest symptom of its return disturbs me more than I can tell you."

"I wish you could both help recollecting. You are so over anxious to make each other happy, so afraid of the least misunderstanding, that it brings an atmosphere of restraint into the house. I have often noticed it. People can't live quite happily together unless they are at the bottom of their hearts at ease with each other."

"We have not been at ease lately; not since you left us. You were the medium that put us in accord. You have a most happy calming power over my mother —over every one who comes near you, I think. What a beautiful gift it is! I am better already for talking to you; if you let us stay here all the evening we shall go home quite well. There, do you hear that? My mother's natural, happy laugh; I have not heard it for a whole week. There is good humour in the very walls of your room; no one can resist it."

Mrs. Edgecombe had not resisted it; the last ten minutes had had a surprising effect in clearing her brow and bringing back her usual frank, cordial manner. "I am laughing over Aunt Bessie's dismay at the prospect of the ball at the Red House, with which Mrs. Franklyn threatens us," she said, gaily, when Clemency turned to ask the cause of her mirth. " I hear that you made quite a fight to prevent our being asked; that you even refused to write the invitation till Mrs. Franklyn sketched out one to write herself, which offended you by its urgency. You were afraid such *empressement* from her would quite turn Walter's head : now, were you not ? "

" Here are your notes," said Clemency, selecting two from a heap of sealed envelopes that lay on a side-table. " You know quite well why I did not want you to be asked, though I don't believe you will mind the being made a ridiculous fuss with, so much as I shall mind seeing it."

" Give the notes to me, Miss Franklyn," cried Colonel Edgecombe, with pretended eagerness. " My mother is capable of putting them into her pocket, and pretending to forget the day ; whereas I feel dismayed to think of your treacherously scheming to deprive me of a ball just from an unworthy dislike of seeing your friends made much of. I wonder you have the face to confess such baseness. I should never have forgiven you if you had carried your point."

" You would never have heard anything about it."

"Indeed but I should. Do you suppose that such an event as a ball at the Red House can even be talked of, without all the birds of the air carrying the matter? It reached me hours ago."

"Then Sydney Serle must have told you. I sent her note yesterday, I was so much afraid Mrs. Franklyn might change her mind about having her."

"You did a kind thing," said Colonel Edgecombe, cordially, "and you would have been rewarded if you had seen the pleasure it gave. Your note of invitation for the ball was as good as a college degree, or an order of knighthood to Miss Serle. Really when one can confer distinction so easily, and put modest little people on a pedestal at such small expense, it would be quite a pity not to do it."

Mrs. Edgecombe had risen to take leave, and was standing with her back to her son and Clemency as they chatted together. They did not see any change in her face, and were both startled by the dry tone of her voice when she addressed them again.

"So you, too, have taken to patronise the Serles, my dear Clemency. They are such very patronisable people, and *do* so bring it on themselves, that I can hardly blame you; but it is not a very wise or safe thing to do. However, if poor little Sydney can really be made quite happy by the prospect of dancing at a ball while her father is overwhelmed with anxiety and trouble, it would be a pity to deny it her. I never thought she had any feeling."

A half-suppressed growl of disapproval from Colonel Edgecombe was audible during this speech, and when it was over he sprang up and began to pace the room again.

Mrs. Edgecombe turned to Miss Arnays, and repeated some last words she had been addressing to her in an ostentatiously gay, indifferent tone.

Clemency stood silent for a minute, looking at the two in dismay, and pondering a resolution. She could not let them go away in that humour with each other.

When Mrs. Edgecombe came near to wish her good-bye, she drew her aside towards the window, and looked up beseechingly in her face.

" Dear Mrs. Edgecombe, please I must say something. You know I don't mean to patronise the Serles; that I never in my life thought of such an impertinent thing as patronising any one. And you know, too, don't you, that Sydney Serle would not really neglect her father for any pleasure ? You are only a little provoked with her sometimes ; you don't really in your heart think her unfeeling. I should be so much obliged to you if you would say this before you go."

" Why should I say it ? "

" Just to satisfy me. You are really so kind, I can't bear that you should even talk as if you ever were unjust to people."

" And I can't bear it either, mother," Colonel Edgecombe said, pausing in his walk close at Clemency's side.

" We are two against you, you see : satisfy us both."

" You both ! Really you are a dutiful son and goddaughter to take me to task in this fashion. Am I always to account for all my inconsiderate words to you two for the future, pray ? "

" Scold me as much as you like for my impertinence, only look at me like yourself," cried Clemency.

" And at me, too, mother," said Colonel Edgecombe.

Mrs. Edgecombe held out a hand to each, and a visible quiver of emotion passed over her face.

" There, there, foolish good children, be satisfied ; you shall order how I am to look and speak. I give in. I will praise every one within fifty miles of Tunstall to please you two. I will think Sydney Serle a sensible girl, and Mrs. Franklyn just what Clemency orders. Will that do ? "

" Dear Mrs. Edgecombe, you are too kind," Clemency

said, while Colonel Edgecombe stooped down and kissed the hand his mother had held out to him.

There was a second's embarrassed pause, then it came into Clemency's head to make some remark about Mrs. Franklyn's preparations for her ball, and in another minute they were all talking eagerly and laughing heartily about nothing, with the wonderful sense of relief and happiness that comes when a little cloud of misunderstanding between close friends has been unexpectedly cleared away. It was Miss Arnays' pity for the drenched horses and servants waiting outside that interrupted the conversation, and obliged Mrs. Edgecombe to take leave at last.

Colonel Edgecombe, after crossing the threshold, turned back and entered the little room once more. There was no occasion for his doing so, for he had already taken leave of both the ladies. Finding himself opposite Clemency, however, he held out his hand and took hers again. "Thank you," he said, emphatically.

It did not take a second the speaking of these two words, the understanding look that went with them, or the hardly completed action of placing a second hand over the one he held. Clemency could almost persuade herself that the second leave-taking was a dream, it passed so quickly; yet she could not deny that the remembrance of it would recur, and that it gave a new colour to her thoughts all the evening. She had been wanted then—she told herself, over and over again; she could be of use to her friends. The life she had been following in thought all this last week had not been complete without her. She wondered whether it was foolish or wrong to find such strange inexpressible sweetness in the thought; to allow the words of undeserved, unnecessary thanks to go on repeating themselves over and over again, a never-ending song in her heart.

CHAPTER VII.

A whisper half revealed her to herself.

Aylmer's Field.

A VISIT to the Red House had been hanging over
Clemency ever since the beginning of the year. It
had at one time been considered a settled thing that
she was to live with her father and step-mother as soon
as her education was finished; but as no one wanted
her at home, and as her aunt's resolution invariably
failed whenever a time for her removal to the Red
House was fixed upon, it had remained a purpose, to
be discussed from time to time, but never carried into
effect.

The Red House stood about a mile and a-half from
Tunstall, on the ugly barren side of the country; out
of reach of the Combe Woods, and in close vicinity to
pit mouths and tall chimneys.

It was a heavy red-brick building, standing at the
top of a bare hill, for the whole neighbourhood to stare
at. Mr. Franklyn had built it a few years ago for his

own occupation, and, more fortunate than most people who meddle with house architecture, he had triumphantly succeeded in satisfying himself. He considered the intense ugliness of his house a testimony to his own good sense, and would really have been ashamed of living in a building that pretended to such a useless merit as looking beautiful outside. He held that a house was a place to eat and sleep in—if it afforded every convenience for enjoying these chief ends of existence luxuriously, what more could be required, except perhaps that it should be large and conspicuous enough to impress passers-by with a sense of its owner's consequence? The spacious gardens round the house were laid out in a style that corresponded with the building, and by dint of formality, want of shade, and glaring combinations of colours, succeeded as nearly as possible in making flower-plots and gravelled walks an offence instead of a pleasure to the eye.

"How glad I am that it is the Red House, not home," Clemency had said to her aunt, just before she started on her drive to Tunstall, and the feeling of self-gratulation recurred when the carriage stopped, and she woke from a pleasant reverie that had lasted through the drive to find herself at her father's door.

Mrs. Franklyn was out driving, and Clemency had

leisure to wander about the house, and compare its luxurious, pretentious unhomeliness with the stately unhomeliness of High Combe in its dreary days, and decide how much more she disliked the one than the other. She would gladly have betaken herself to the nursery, the only room in the house to which she was cordially welcomed ; but Mrs. Franklyn was a strict disciplinarian, and would have resented any interruption of the children's daily routine.

Contrary to Clemency's past experience, however, the waiting hour was the most disagreeable one she had to endure. Mrs. Franklyn returned from her drive in an unusually amiable mood, and surprised Clemency by the cordiality of her greeting. It was more than kind. There was a disposition to make much of her, and treat her with quite a new sort of consideration, which was very puzzling indeed to Clemency.

"What can be the matter with me ?" Clemency asked herself, as she hastened through her evening toilette ; "I must have changed somehow. If my step-mother takes to making much of me, I shall grow puzzled about myself. I looked in the glass several times to be quite sure that I was not Mrs. Edgecombe. Well, it is pleasant to be tolerated, for whatever reason ; and now—for the best hour of a Red House day."

The best hour was the one before dinner, when the four younger children came down into the drawing-room to see their father. Mr. Franklyn showed much more affection to the children of his second marriage than he had ever done to his elder son and daughter, who had been separated from him during a great part of their childhood, and to whom he had never since become accustomed.

Clemency was not jealous of this preference; on the contrary, the sight of her father's affection for her young sisters always gave her a hope for her brother and herself. When she saw him bend his stiff figure and relax his grave face to listen to their prattle, a strong yearning to win her right place in his heart rose up, and she forgot the dividing influence that had always hitherto kept them asunder.

The youngest child, a boy of two years old, was seated on Clemency's knee, and the three little girls were standing round listening open-mouthed to a story about Colonel Edgecombe killing a snake in the Combe Woods, when she heard her father's slow step approaching the drawing-room. From her childhood, this sound had always made her heart beat quickly, not with fear but with expectation, always disappointed but never quite extinguished. She felt that if she could meet her father just a little differently—if he would but once

look at her with a different expression in his eyes, or
if she could ever so little alter the tone of her voice in
speaking the first word to him, the barrier of reserve
between them might fall down, and they might be
what other fathers and daughters were to each other.
She always felt this with an agony of longing before he
entered the room, and then, when her eyes met his,
she found the same cold impenetrable look in them
which always seemed to put her so very far away, and
the usual stiff questions and shy answers followed. She
had resolved to make a great effort to-day; but she was
once more disappointed in herself. The children were
not as helpful to the conversation as she had expected;
they were too full of her story to care for their father's
notice, and he soon withdrew from them, and took up his
usual position upright before the chimney-piece, with his
back to the fire. Clemency stole wistful glances at his
face in the pauses of her story. It was not an easy one
to read. His thin lips rested on each other, always in
the same firm line, suggestive of habitual silence; his
grey eyes looked out with the same apparent indifference as to what they saw; yet Clemency fancied she
discerned an additional shade of dissatisfaction on his
face that day, and as she had learned from long observation to connect that particular look with some real

or supposed misdeed of her brother's, she longed impatiently for the first time in her life to be alone with her mother, that she might question her on the subject.

The dinner hour seemed interminable. Her father maintained a moody silence while it lasted, and her mother plied her with minute questions about the changes which Colonel Edgecombe's return had effected at High Combe; the number of times she had dined there while Lord and Lady St. Erme had been visiting their sister, Mrs. Edgecombe, and precisely how Lady St. Erme was dressed on each occasion. As soon as she and Mrs. Franklyn were alone together Clemency asked anxiously,

"Has papa had a letter from Dr. Bromley about Rolla this morning?"

"Now, Clemency, how could you have guessed it? You are as bad as Rolla himself for finding out what one is thinking about. I declare it makes me quite uncomfortable. I think there is something uncanny about you both."

"No, I am only uncanny where Rolla and papa are concerned. So there has been a letter. I do think if Dr. Bromley knew how papa broods over and exaggerates every word, and how unhappy it makes him, he would not write so many complaining letters; for after all they are only about trifles."

"I don't know what you call trifles, Clemency. Your father desired me to write and beg Dr. Bromley to be candid, and I only did what he told me," Mrs. Franklyn said, a slight compunction of conscience leading her to inculpate herself unawares. "You and your aunt always seem to think somehow that I am to blame for your father's dissatisfaction with Rolla; but you ought to know that it's doing him no kindness to conceal his faults."

"And what did Dr. Bromley say?"

"The old story about Rolla's idleness, and you can't be surprised that your father is seriously annoyed."

"No, I am not surprised, only—poor Rolla, we always knew that he was idle; he never has been anything else. I never expected that going to Dr. Bromley's would cure him quite."

"I expected he would have been grateful, and made an effort to profit by such an advantage."

"I am not sure that it is an advantage to Rolla; he would have been very grateful if papa would have let him have his great wish, and go into the Indian army."

"A most unreasonable wish, indeed; however, I acquit Rolla of having originated it. It was you and Mrs. Edgecombe together who put it into his head a year ago, by talking perpetually about the Indian victories, and reading out all Colonel Edgecombe's letters to him. He has never settled to anything sensible since. You will repent some day that you were ever so foolish as to puff him up with such notions."

Clemency was repenting already. Past conversations with her brother recurred to her mind, and she acknowledged that it certainly was she who invented all the schemes for Rolla's life, and that he was apt to listen with the same acquiescing smile in his beautiful lazy brown eyes, whether she made him a General, or an author, raised him to the woolsack, or suffered him to perish in an unsuccessful attempt to cut through the Isthmus of Panama. One story was as agreeable as another to Rolla.

"Was there anything besides complaints in Dr. Bromley's letter?" she asked after a pause. "Any praise to sweeten it?"

"Not a word that could sweeten it to your father. Dr. Bromley remarked, as he always does, on Rolla's good humour and disposition to make friends with every one he meets, and ended with the old assurance that idleness and childishness are his worst faults. As if he could possibly have any worse, any more utterly aggravating to his father. His very good humour is an aggravation. I am sure I have often been so provoked to see him coming smiling into this room of an evening when his father had been finding fault with him all day, that I would have given anything to see him sulky, as any other boy would have been. How we are to get on when he comes to live at home, and has to go every day with your father to business, I can't imagine."

"Do you mean that my father is thinking of that? It will never do. Oh, mother, do try to prevent it!"

The entreating tone touched Mrs. Franklyn's heart, by no means a bad one at the bottom.

"I am ready to do all I can for Rolla," she said; "but what other plan can I propose? Dr. Bromley's letter has decided your father not to send him to college, and I dare not at present suggest the army again. Your father has said once that it is out of the question for Rolla. Of course he never talks about the state of his affairs to me, he never talks about anything; but I can see he has many anxieties weighing on his mind. I heard to-day that water had come again into the Red Hill Mine. There always seems to be either fire or water in Mr. Franklyn's mines, and one never hears of such accidents at Vale Combe. I think the Wilsons must contrive it somehow to spite us. By the way, have you heard that young Mr. Wilson is going to take Arthur Yonge into partnership?"

" Arthur Yonge was saying something of the kind to Aunt Bessie a few nights ago ; but I am afraid I did not listen very attentively. I think Arthur was not sanguine, because Mr. Wilson wanted money, and Arthur has none. Still there was a hope. Arthur has a scheme for extracting more or better iron from the iron stone than any one has ever done before, and Mr. Wilson is enterprising, and is disposed to try his plan. I hope it will succeed, though perhaps I ought not ; for if it does, the Vale Combe Mines will flourish instead of ours, and we shall have to come down in the world as old Mr. Yonge did long ago. It will be our turn."

" Really, Clemency, you are as childish as Rolla ; there is no talking seriously to you. I am shocked to hear that Arthur Yonge has the baseness even to think he has invented a way of making other people's iron better than Mr. Franklyn's. Why it would be actually robbing us, and after all your aunt's kindness to him. It just shows what a bad heart he has."

" What a good head he has, we should have said, if it had been Rolla who had invented anything. Perhaps papa would have been proud and fond of him if he had. I am afraid I have a bad heart ; for I believe I am actually grudging Arthur his cleverness, and wishing that Rolla could have it instead."

"How you do run from one extreme to another, Clemency—one moment wanting the whole family to be sacrificed to Rolla, and the next putting him on a par with Arthur Yonge."

"I only wish I could, at least if Rolla is to come home and work with papa. I like my own good-humoured, lazy, beautiful Rolla best for myself; but when it comes to papa having anything to do with him, the more like Arthur Yonge he grows the better for us all. Can nothing be said to dissuade papa from bringing Rolla to live at home?"

"I can't interfere; but it is not to be for three months, and before then something may have happened that would give you a right to advise. One ought not to speak of such things prematurely, certainly; but I could not help reflecting to-day that possibly before the end of the summer something may have fallen out that will dispose your father to listen more favourably to talk of Rolla's going into the army, than he would now. You don't take me into your confidence, Clemency; but I can't shut my eyes and ears to what is going on, and I assure you that no one will rejoice in your good fortune more than I shall. It will put you in a position to be of great service to Rolla, and by-and-by, when your sisters begin to grow up, I shall expect—"

"But what do you mean?" cried Clemency. How can I serve Rolla by the end of the summer better than now? Why should papa listen to me then?"

"Well, things happen. People's positions change. One can't help looking forward when everything points so clearly one way—your being asked so often to meet the St. Ermes, and all."

For a minute longer Clemency looked in her mother's face with amazed unconscious eyes, and then the blood crimsoned her face, and she turned away vexed with herself, for the suspicion of Mrs. Franklyn's meaning that had come to her.

Mrs. Franklyn laughed drily.

"You need not be so very reserved with me, my dear, seeing I am your mother," she said. "Besides, I believe I was the first person to notice anything. The day when we all dined at High Combe, and Colonel Edgecombe sat next you at dinner, I told your father, as we were driving home, that I knew how it would end. It is plain enough to see that your aunt and Mrs. Edgecombe have planned it all along."

"Oh mother, I wish you had not said this. You can't think how sorry I am that you have said it."

There was so much real pain and dismay in Clemency's voice that Mrs. Franklyn was obliged to assume an injured tone to reinstate herself in her usual self-complacency.

"And pray why may not I say what every one in the neighbourhood has been saying for the last two months? Am I the only person to be kept in the dark, or do you expect all the Tunstall people to believe that Colonel Edgecombe rides every day to Tunstall for nothing but to dig in your aunt's garden? It is quite absurd to make a secret of what every one is gossiping about."

"But there is no secret, believe me," Clemency said.

Mrs. Franklyn laughed provokingly.

"Well, well, as you please. I really did not mean to distress you so terribly, my dear. I know it is not right to look forward, and I dare say your aunt has cautioned you against being too sure. If it were not that Mrs. Edgecombe's wishes are so clear, I should have said it was almost too good a match for you to aspire to. But there, you need not throw your head up and look so haughty; I will say no more. Your father is coming up-stairs. Go to the piano, and give us some music, or he will wonder what you have been doing to give your cheeks such a colour."

For the rest of the evening Clemency kept herself from thinking by playing over all the most difficult pieces she could find in her portfolio. It was not till she was safe in her own room at night, and had put out her candle, that she trusted herself to recall her mother's words. In the dark, with the cool night air from the open window blowing over her face, it did not signify how much her cheeks burned ; and she might try to find out what it was that had made her so wonderfully angry ; and endeavour, as she had often done before, to take the thorns out of her mind, which a conversation with her mother had planted there.

For a time the task seemed vain. The longer she thought about it the more indignant she grew. Hot tears gathered in her eyes, and, falling slowly, made her burning cheeks hotter than ever. It seemed so very hard, so cruel, that people who knew nothing about her should interfere with idle gossip, and spoil a happiness and content they could not possibly understand. She felt as if she could never look her two friends at High Combe in the face again without shame, now she knew how people were speaking of her and them. For two months, too—all the happy golden days of those two bright spring months had been counted by other people as well as by herself; they would never seem quite her own again. It was terrible to know that all the marks of peculiar friendship, which she had hardly

trusted herself to think about because they were too
precious to be looked at, had been commented upon,
watched, and even made by her stepmother a ground
for calculating future advantages. For a while she
thought it was all spoilt for her—the sweet spring time,
the delightful rambles, the gay work together, the long,
intimate, friendly conversations, in which she knew now
she had shown more of her inmost thoughts than she
had ever put into words before. They had all been so
beautiful, and now the glory was lifted away from them,
and they were reduced to every-day world events, about
which people could make the speculations, and talk the
kind of gossip she had always so hated.

The future was still worse to contemplate. She
could never be happy and at ease at Combe again ;
there must be an end of all true freedom and intimacy.
It would not do to have such cruel things said of her
aunt and Mrs. Edgecombe. To vindicate them from the
odium of having made such a plan for her, she must
give up the pleasantest friendship she had ever had in
her life, just, too, when she was becoming fit to profit
by it—just, too, when the hope had dawned on her that
the advantage was not all on her side, that she might
possibly be of some consequence to her friend. When
she reached this point Clemency's face dropped into her

hands, and the fast-gathering tears had their way. They did her good. Somehow or other, when she lifted up her head again all the bitterness and regret and pain were washed out of her heart. She was no longer angry with herself or any one. She leaned out towards the open window. The soft west wind blew over her, bringing scents of flowers from the garden below. An indescribable sense of refreshment, strength, exaltation came to her with it, reversing her former mood. She wondered why she had wept—what the strange spasm of pain had meant. Had it in passing left a new joy behind? How could she be unhappy on a still June night like this, with the wind blowing from Combe to her, laden with the perfume of early summer flowers, which she fancied would always bring her such happy memories?—sweet summer woods, sweet flowers, sweet memories, of which no one should rob her. She felt strong enough to defend them now. One by one the incidents of the past weeks rose up like pictures before her mental eye, distincter, fuller of meaning than they had seemed an hour or two ago. Significant, joyful remarks of Mrs. Edgecombe's, admiring looks, words which came back with the very accent they had been uttered in—she had not known before how deeply they had graven themselves on her memory; she was half frightened at the discovery now. She wished it had come through any other way than through words of Mrs. Franklyn's; but since it had come she would not be so cowardly as to turn away. For good or ill, she had looked into her heart, and discovered what was in it—for good or ill—for great joy or bitterest pain. She bowed down her head on her clasped hands again as the alternative rose before her. Even the soft moonlight was too glaring, the gentle wind too intrusive for the mood it brought. When she could look up again she felt as if a great wave of time had broken over her head, bearing her away from her proud, confident, careless girlhood to a new standing-point, from which, yet distant and dim, the great possible joys and sorrows of a woman's life were visible.

CHAPTER VIII.

Es gibt im Menschenleben Augenblicke,
Wo er dem Weltgeist näher ist als sonst,
Und eine Frage frei hat an das Schicksal.
Wallenstein.

THE miser's house at Tunstall was a somewhat less disagreeable abode in summer than in winter. In the wide empty rooms, fresh air and sunlight were to be had without cost, and Mr. Yonge could find no pretext for grudging them to himself or his household. He generally brightened up a little, held his head more erect, and lost something of his careworn expression, when the mild weather and the lengthening days relieved him from the daily torture of watching the consumption of fuel and candles, which Arthur would not allow him to restrict beyond a certain point while the winter lasted. The spring that year wrought a marked change in him. The old servant told Arthur that her master was more like himself than he had been for twenty years. Arthur had no recollection of

that brighter better self to which she referred; but it
was a very great happiness to him when his grandfather's resumption of former habits and partially-
restored intelligence made companionship between
them possible. His life at home had been so singularly solitary hitherto, and he had such a craving
for sympathy and family affection, that the slight
improvement seemed a great boon to him,—greater
that spring than it would have been at any other time,
for it gave a new turn to his thoughts just when they
were disposed to dwell morbidly on one subject. When
he passed the gate of Miss Arnays' little garden, and
perceived that his usual spring work there was in the
course of being performed by other hands, it consoled
him a little to remember that his grandfather was
anxiously awaiting his return, to take his evening
walk, and that he depended on him for the one pleasant hour of his weary day.

Few people would have agreed with Arthur in
finding the garrulous rambling talk which Mr. Yonge
poured forth during these evening walks, preferable
to the old sad silence. The old man's mind was
not at all times equally clear. Arthur attributed
the change in his habits to a gradual restoration
of his impaired mental faculties, but it was in reality

caused merely by an alteration in the nature of his delusions. His thoughts about the present were as clouded and unreal as ever ; but he had for the time escaped from the present, and was living in a more or less connected dream of the past. He constantly mistook Arthur for his son (Arthur's father), and appealed to his recollection of events that had happened before he was born. He interested himself very much now in watching Arthur's chemical experiments, and in drawing from him a detailed account of the business in which he had been engaged during the day. But even while he seemed most thoroughly to understand the matter in hand, he would use a name or refer to a locality which showed it was the world of twenty-five years ago, and the men of a past generation, whose affairs he believed himself to be discussing.

During these conversations Arthur learned more about his father's life, about the aims he had set before him, and the plans he had, with more or less success, begun to carry out, than he had ever before had an opportunity of knowing. All he heard made a great impression upon him ; he had had many schemes and ambitions of his own ; when he heard what his father's had been, he was struck with their greater di-interestedness. His father's projects might have been visionary, ill-fitted for the time or place, or rashly entered upon ; but at least their purport showed that it was not for self-aggrandisement, or in the hope of heaping up wealth, that their originator had studied and toiled and risked so much. From poring over these schemes, many grave questions hitherto unheeded began to occupy Arthur's mind, wider sympathies and higher views of duty and responsibility dawned upon him, and his castles in the air were less limited and self-involved than they had formerly been. For the last few months a prospect of advancement had opened before him, which gave him greater excuse than he had formerly had for indulging in visions.

Mr. Wilson, the head of the firm in which he was employed, had died during the winter, and had been succeeded by his son, an old schoolfellow of Arthur's, who had always been a great adherent of his and a firm believer in the importance of his discovery. He had offered to take Arthur into partnership, and to give him the opportunity of trying his new method of purifying the crude iron, if he could furnish a certain portion of the money necessary for the first outlay. This did not seem an unreasonable demand to young Wilson, for almost every one in Tunstall believed

that Mr. Yonge had considerable sums of money
hoarded away. His wife had had a small fortune,
which had not been swallowed up in the bankruptcy,
and his extraordinarily penurious manner of living
for many years had filled his neighbours' minds with
vague notions of his accumulated wealth. Mr. Yonge
had always kept Arthur in complete ignorance of his
resources, if he had any ; and the smallest allusion to
his supposed hoards threw him into such an agony of
terror that Arthur was extremely unwilling to ask a
question, or make a remark likely to turn his thoughts
in that direction. A few weeks before this time, when
his hopes had first been excited by his friend's pro-
posal, he had taken some pains to bring the facts of
the case before his grandfather, and make him look at
them as present realities, instead of recollections of past
events. He succeeded better than he had expected in
securing his grandfather's attention, but the effect produced on the old man's mind by the breaking up of his
illusions was so painful that Arthur regretted having
done anything to bring it about. The suspicious temper and abject groundless fears, from which he had been
lately relieved, returned in greater force than ever, and
with them symptoms of restlessness and mental struggle,
which Arthur had never observed in him before.

Two or three times during the rainy days which had
been so tedious to Clemency, Arthur, on coming home
for the evening, heard from their old servant that his
grandfather had been absent from the house during
several hours of the day, apparently wandering about
aimlessly in the rain.   Once Arthur had to go
and look for him, and after an hour's search he found
him about two miles from Tunstall, on the Combe
road, sitting wearily to rest on a mile-stone, with his
head bowed between his hands, and seeming quite
unaware of the soft falling rain, that dripped slowly
from his white hair and threadbare coat to the sodden
ground.   The dejected air of his whole figure, and the
expression of miserable perplexity on his face when he
raised it at the sound of approaching steps, gave Arthur
a shock of painful pity, which he could not forget for
many days.   He had been, from earliest childhood, so
accustomed to his grandfather's condition, that it was
only now, when these changes of mood directed his
thoughts more constantly towards him, that he quite
understood how pitiable a state it was, or fully realized
the gloom cast over his own life, and the extent of the
sacrifices he was daily called upon to make.

On the evening of the day Clemency went to the
Red House, Arthur passed a painful hour revolv-

ing these thoughts in his mind. A fruitless hour he knew it would be, bringing weakness rather than strength, as self-pitying moods always do. He resolved several times to rouse himself, and resume his interrupted studies, but his candle had burned down in the socket and gone out; he was not sure that the house would afford another, and he felt indisposed for the exertion of going to look;—besides, the moonlight had tempted him to the open window, and the thoughts, painful as they were, had a sort of attraction that tempted him to follow where they led. Sad thoughts have a fashion of approaching sometimes with gentlest alluring aspect, and when the unwary heart has opened wide to take them in, and surrendered itself powerless to their sway, they slip off the disguise, and prove their power to torture or dismay.

Arthur had had a conversation that morning with his friend, in which the advantages of the proposed partnership had been still more clearly pointed out to him, and he had been urged strongly to do all he could to persuade his grandfather to open his hoards and furnish him with the necessary help. Arthur was now convinced that his grandfather did not lack the power to place him in the position he coveted, only the will. And as picture after picture

rose up before his mind, of the unnecessary privations, the petty, sordid cares and humiliations that
had embittered all his life hitherto, a hot feeling
of indignation rose up, and for the first time he asked
himself, must this longer be borne ? Must he lose
every chance in life, and pass all his young years in the
miserable task of protecting a half-insane man from his
own delusions ? Would it not be right to make one
more effort to induce his grandfather to act reasonably,
and if it failed leave Tunstall for ever, and seek his
fortunes elsewhere ? The world beyond Tunstall looked
very tempting to him as the prospect rose. In a new
place he should no longer have to combat the prejudices
which his grandfather's conduct raised against him ;
his talents would have freer scope, and there would
no longer be the depressing sight of such a home as
this to weigh him down.

While his mind was revolving these thoughts,
Arthur's ear caught the sound of his grandfather's
feeble steps pacing restlessly up and down the room
above. He interrupted his thoughts to listen to the
unequal footfalls, now quick, now slow, now pausing
an instant, now hurrying on with feverish haste—
his heart sank as he heard, and he had a sensation of
positive physical pain, as if he felt the restless tottering

steps trampling over him ; for in the utter helplessness
and misery of which they were tokens he recognised a
claim he could not withstand, a claim to which he knew
all his own hopes and purposes in life would have to
be sacrificed. If it had been a person as strong as himself who had opposed his purposes, he could have
struggled for what he thought were his own rights, but
it was not in him either to oppress and overrule one so
feeble as his grandfather, or to abandon him in his
forlorn dependence. He estimated fully the suffering
of the slavery to which he resigned himself, he was
not sure that there might not be more wisdom in the
harsher course, but he knew once for all that he should
not take it. Reverence and pity were too strong in
him,—he did not call his feeling by these names, he
was half angry, half contemptuous with himself for
what he believed a want of power to act reasonably,—
he only knew that some power within him forbad his
carrying out his half-formed purpose, and that he must
turn again and take up the burden he had all but
resolved to throw down.

Unwillingly, painfully, grudgingly, he made the
silent sacrifice, seeing the life spread out before,
as dark and bitter as exaggerating youthful fancy
could paint it. The soft night winds blowing from

the Combe Woods seemed to burn his face as he
leaned towards the window, the flickering light on the
sky tortured his eyes. He thought he hated Combe
and Tunstall and all the familiar scenes he could see
from his high window,—above all he hated the life he
saw himself wearing away among them—a life passed
in humble work which gave little scope for the faculties he felt he possessed; in watching the gradual
darkening of the one life to which ties of kindred
bound him; in seeing familiar friends lifted up into
positions from which they would look down in scorn on
him, (the plural words came even in thought, but there
was only one figure present in his mind,)—it all lay
before him, and he knew that he should stay and meet
it—he should not shirk any of the labour and pain,—it
was there for him to go through, and hate it as he
might, an influence within stronger than his own self-
will would not let him turn away. No particular result
came from that unspoken resolve, and yet the moment
of taking it was a turning point in Arthur's life; one of
those pregnant moments when the course of the future
development of a character towards good or evil is
determined, perhaps for ever.

For some time Arthur was so absorbed in the
conflict going on in his mind, that he ceased to be con-

scious of outward sounds. There was a pause unnoticed by him in the footsteps overhead; the door of his room stood open, and it was not till he felt a trembling hand laid on his shoulder, and heard his name spoken in his ear, that he turned round and saw by the faint light that his grandfather was standing beside him in the window-recess. He was not much surprised, for Mr. Yonge had a habit of wandering about the house at night, but when the old man took a step forward, and the moonlight fell full on his face, Arthur was struck by its agitated expression; the cheeks were flushed, and the sunken eyes burnt with a feverish light. He had a small box, padlocked, in his hand, which he held out tremblingly to Arthur.

"There," he said, in a frightened eager whisper, "take it and hide it quick; never let any one know that I had it, or mention it to me again."

"What has happened to disturb you?" Arthur said. "You have no cause for fear, or for hiding anything; there is no one here but you and me."

"She was here a minute ago, Arthur—your mother, and she is angry with me. She looked just as she used to look years ago, when you were a boy, and I refused to give you something she thought you ought to have. There, when I give you all I have, she will be satisfied.   I have been saving it up for you for years and years; I always meant it for you when the right time came, and she says it has come now."

Arthur took the box from the old man's hand, seeing he had hardly strength to hold it, and placed it on a table near.

"There is no one angry with you," he said soothingly, "and no one has a right to order you to give your money to me unless you like."

"Yes, she has, Arthur.   She used to say sometimes that your plans failed because I did not help you enough; but if I give you all, she can never reproach me again; and, perhaps, she will come back to stay here always, not just to look in at doors and windows, and glide away as she does now.   When I first began to put the money away, she was pleased; she liked as well as I did to see it grow, knowing that I meant it all for you; but now when I take it out to count it, she stands before me frowning, and I have no peace. . . Don't unlock the box till I have gone, and don't begin to count the notes and sovereigns, or you will go on doing it all night as I often do.   There is all I have saved, and the money I lent Mr. Serle, which I have made him give back to me.   I told him she wanted it for you, and

he was obliged to let me have it then. Now let me
go upstairs again; I feel better, and think I can go to
sleep."

Arthur led the old man upstairs, and helped him to
bed, and stayed with him as long as his agitation lasted.
Sometimes he tried gently to lead his thoughts away
from the fancies that filled his mind, but on the whole
he found it better to listen quietly.

"You, Arthur, are the only one of them all who stays
with me," Mr. Yonge kept saying; "the others come
and go, and keep away a long time if I do or think anything to vex them; but you are always here, always
with me. There is something about that in the Bible,—
'thee have I always with me, and all that I have is
thine'—now I have given you all, you will stay always,
won't you?"

He fell asleep at last, and Arthur returned to his
own room, too weary to think much over what had
passed. The next morning Mr. Yonge did not come
downstairs as usual, he had a slight attack of fever,
and was confined to his bed for several days. His
thoughts wandered, and he talked almost incessantly to
himself during his illness, but his fancies were all
gentle and tender now, fear and sordid cares about
money no longer mixed with them. Arthur took advan-

tage of his unconsciousness to introduce many little comforts into his room which had long been absent from it, and, aided by the old servant's recollections, he restored the rest of the house to something like its former condition. When his grandfather's health allowed him to come downstairs again, Arthur watched anxiously the effect the changed aspect of the rooms produced upon him. It was very different from what it would have been a few months before. He had grown much feebler, and seemed many years older than before his short illness. His quick observation and restless anxiety about trifles had left him, and he hardly seemed to notice what went on around him. Now and then his eye rested wistfully on one or another of the new objects near him, but oftenest he would sit for hours quite still in his chair, with his eyes fixed wistfully on the door, as if he expected it to open and admit some one.

When Arthur entered, a faint smile always dawned on his face. "Yes, you always come," he would say, "you never keep me very long waiting. I wish I knew as well when to expect the others; everything about the house looks now as if they ought always to be here, and sometimes they do come and look at me, but they are not to be depended upon like you."

It was a melancholy greeting enough. Yet Arthur learned to care very much for it. It was the only sort of home-welcome he had ever known in his life, or for years was to know.

The Tunstall gossips would have been disappointed if they had ever been made aware of the comparatively small amount of Mr. Yonge's hoards. They were, however, large enough to secure the accomplishment of Arthur's plans, and place him in a position which six months ago he would have considered wholly unattainable.

CHAPTER IX.

Sweet, thou hast trod on a heart.
Pass! there's a world full of men;
And women as fair as thou art
Must do such things now and then.
Thou only hast stepped unaware.
Malice, not one can impute;
And why should a heart have been there,
In the way of a fair woman's foot?

VALE COMBE Manor House wore its loveliest aspect in the early months of the year, the garden in front was so full of spring flowers and early-blooming shrubs; the orchard behind so glorious with its show of delicate pink and white blossoms; the little river, replenished by the winter's rain, ran over its stony bed with such a brisk merry chatter; the great trees of the Combe Woods on the hill above, while their stalwart arms still showed distinct amid a mist of softest green, enclosed the little valley in such a perfect setting; that it was difficult to imagine a spot which could suggest a deeper sense of security and peace. It was no wonder that people from Tunstall and Hemsley, who had any acquaintance with the Serles, were ready to invent excuses for paying them frequent visits, and spending long afternoons cowslipping in the river fields, or tea-drinking in the orchard during this pleasantest season of the whole year.

These visitors were chiefly acquaintances made of late years by George Serle, or connections of his wife's, and were a grade or two lower in the social scale than the friends with whom Mr. Serle had associated in his prosperous days; but since they came to admire the farm, and enjoy the spring beauty which was filling all his heart with gladness, the kindly old man never failed to give them an eager welcome, and took great pride and delight in pointing out the prettiest views, and in sending them back to their town homes laden with tokens of the spring.

Mrs. George Serle, indeed, could be irate now and then against people who thoughtlessly interrupted the farm work at busy seasons, caused stores of cream to be invaded, and made off with pats of golden butter which they might just as well have bought in Hemsley on the next market-day; but as the delinquents were mostly her own old associates, she bottled up her anger and grudging for private family use, and seconded her husband's and father's lavish hospitality with such show of grim tolerance as was possible to her. To Sydney any event was dearly welcome which broke into the routine of her life, and gave her an excuse for spending idle hours out in the sunshine, with faces she did not see every day round her and admiring eyes following her about. Occasionally it is true a little fit of disdain would come over her, if she had been spending the previous day at High Combe, or had met Mrs. Edgecombe in her morning walk, and by way of variety she would hold herself aloof from her sister's guests, and affect to look down on their amusements. But the pretence seldom lasted her through a whole afternoon. Talking and laughing had a magnetic effect to draw her into their neighbourhood, and she could no more help making herself the centre of attraction when holiday-making was going on, than the butterflies in the sheltered garden nooks could help being drawn out to flutter in the spring sunshine. Her occasional reserve had no other effect than that of impressing her acquaintances with a vague notion of her superiority, and making her various lovers doubly grateful for the gracious words and smiles she vouchsafed at the end of the evening, in atonement for the scornful airs with which she had bewildered them a few hours before.

Such of the visitors at Vale Combe as were interested enough in Sydney to watch her narrowly, had reason this spring to complain of greater changeableness and occasional worse treatment than they had ever had to put up with before. That bright season was not a very happy time to Sydney. There was as much activity in the farm-house as in former years; as many visitors came; and as many expeditions were planned to the Combe Woods; but Sydney was now far less frequently in a mood to join them. The disinclination for society which she had formerly affected was, more or less, real this year. She had two grievances to brood over, which seemed to herself quite excuse enough for any degree of misanthropy.

The one oftenest in her thoughts, but never spoken about, was the comparative neglect with which during the last three months she had been treated by the family at High Combe. She often said to herself that events were falling out just as she had pictured them when she stood at the window, on the rainy afternoon after Colonel Edgecombe's arrival at Combe. High Combe was not any further from Vale Combe than it used to be, neither was there any marked change in the intercourse between their inmates. Mrs. Edgecombe sent down books and newspapers for old Mr.

Serle as regularly as ever, and had as many cordial pleasant words to give Sydney when they chanced to meet
in the woods or on the Combe Road; yet Sydney felt
as if an impassable chill barrier had suddenly sprung
up between herself and her godmother, which shut her
out from High Combe and all the interests and pleasures once centred there as effectually as if the place
had been spirited away to another quarter of the globe.
It would in reality have been far better for her if it
had been moved away, for then she would have had no
temptation to spend idle hours in trying to make out
the lines of the roof and chimneys through the thickening
foliage of the trees, and in speculating on the occupations
of the inhabitants, till the place began to look to her
like an Eden from which she was unjustly exiled.

The second grievance was one which a very little resolution on her part would have ended at once. It was the
increased intimacy with the Humphreys family perse-
veringly thrust upon her by her sister, and the now
constant visits of Mr. Humphreys in the character of
her acknowledged admirer. There had been no formal
declaration or acceptance; but it had come to be considered an established fact by both families that he was
an encouraged suitor, and Sydney had not courage to
make her own views about the matter clear. Indeed, she

was not always quite sure what her own wishes were. The Misses Humphreys and their grave, imposing-looking brother were very kind to her, and if she was a little overawed by their loud voices and decided manners, she had the satisfaction of seeing that her sister-in-law was even more subdued in their presence than she was. Since she could not shine in the light of Mrs. Edgecombe's countenance, it was something to have the approbation of people as confident in their own opinion as were the Humphreys, to set against her sister-in-law's constant blame. Besides, in spite of his pompous manner and matter-of-fact mode of expressing himself, Sydney had discovered that Mr. Humphreys did really love her—more than her father loved her—more than she could at all understand one person loving another. The discovery caused her more fear than gratification, yet it interested her, and woke a cruel sort of curiosity in her mind—such interest and curiosity as a child (not absolutely cruel but only ignorant) takes in witnessing the struggles of an animal whose sufferings it does not in the smallest degree realise or understand.

Seeing the great effect which kind or unkind words of hers had on the tall, grave, middle-aged man, she could not resist the temptation of experimenting a little with her power, and when her sister

thwarted her will roughly, or taunted her with the
defection of her High Combe friends, she found a sort
of compensation in showing off his entire subjection.
She could not help being glad that Lizzie should see
how thankful he was to be entrusted with commissions
by her, however much they interfered with important
business; and how recklessly he would keep his patients waiting when she chose to encourage him in
dawdling away the best part of a morning in the Vale
Combe orchard. It is true that Mr. Humphreys, after
thus serving as a trophy, had to undergo a proportional
amount of snubbing on his next visit; but then Sydney's highest effort at disdain never succeeded in being
very chilling, and she seldom had resolution to perse-
vere in being cross for a whole evening. When her
sister had gone up-stairs to put the children to bed,
and her father was asleep in his chair, and she had
taken her work to the window, if Mr. Humphreys liked
to come and talk to her, she found it more convenient
to sit still and listen quietly, and make little acquiescing sounds in answer to his long speeches, than to
risk Lizzie's anger by getting up and leaving the room.
Poor Mr. Humphreys could not possibly divine that
while he was pulling an apple-blossom or a cowslip to
pieces, and explaining the difference between the bo-

tanical systems of Linnæus and Lindley, she was softly
saying to herself,—" It is seven o'clock now ; they are
just going in to dinner at High Combe ; I wonder
whether they are sitting in the great or the little
dining-room, and what they are talking to each other
about ?"—or, that when her attention was by chance
directed to him, she was not employed in drinking in
the information he imparted with so much exactness,
but in wondering why he pronounced some of his
words so differently from Mrs. and Colonel Edgecombe ;
or in noting silently the size and clumsiness of the
hands that pulled the delicate flower to pieces, and the
bald patch at the top of his head which he believed he
had concealed satisfactorily by a careful arrangement of
his scanty hair.

Being, fortunately, ignorant of all this, Mr. Humphreys
generally rode home from Vale Combe through the
summer twilight in a very happy frame of mind, feeling thankful that he had acquired such an elegant
science as botany to discourse to young ladies upon,
since he could not edify them with descriptions of
interesting medical cases ; and Sydney meanwhile was
going upstairs to bed with a perplexed and heavy heart.
She saw plainly enough where the events of each day
were leading her, but having no definite purpose or even

wish, she found a sort of relief in letting herself be drifted to a decision by small circumstances, no one of which seemed important enough to dispute about. The lot that did look desirable and glorious in her eyes, seemed also so very far away, so immeasurably distant and unattainable, that no hope of reaching it mixed with, or in the remotest degree influenced, her thoughts of the future. Yet, unhoped-for, this fancied glorious lot was still before her, casting its great shadow over every other earthly object of desire, and making them all look alike unworthy of being sought for or struggled against.

It must be conceded, however, in excuse for Sydney's folly, that even if she had been disposed to put High Combe and the grievance of Mrs. Edgecombe's neglect out of her thoughts, she would have had little chance of succeeding at that time, for all the conversation that went on round her tended to foster her pre-occupation. Every member of the Vale Combe party, from old Mr. Serle to the youngest of his grandchildren, was infected with the enthusiasm for Colonel Edgecombe, that was just then the prevalent popular feeling about Combe; and they were all more or less disposed to boast of tokens of friendliness from him, which seemed to come abundantly to every member of the family except Sydney. In old times it had been Sydney who was distinguished, and the others neglected. Now it was their turn. At every family gathering there was something to tell; some chance encounter with Colonel Edgecombe to relate, or some little act of kindness bestowed by him on some one, to comment upon. He had met George Serle in the woods with his gun, and taken him back to lunch at High Combe; or he had fallen in with the children and given each of the boys a ride down Combe lane on his horse; or come across Mrs. George marketing at Hemsley, and gone into the jeweller's shop with her to explain how old Mr. Serle's broken spectacles might best be mended.

Adventures of this kind so rarely occurred to Sydney that she was disposed at times to fancy herself under a kind of ban, and to believe that Colonel Edgecombe purposely avoided her. Perhaps she had unknowingly done something to displease Mrs. Edgecombe, and Colonel Edgecombe excluded her from the friendliness he entertained toward the rest of the family, to show that he shared his mother's opinion of her. At times Sydney made herself miserable with this supposition, but with all her inclination to see the worst side, it would not always look reasonable. After that, one day in March, when Colonel Edgecombe came upon her unawares in the lane, as she was bending down a branch of catkins from

the hedge to let the youngest child feel its downy
yellow tassels, she could not bring herself to believe
that there was any deep displeasure in his mind towards
her. From the expression of his face, when, at some
slight sound she had turned quickly round, and found
him standing behind her, she could not help thinking
that he must have been looking very kindly either at
the child, or the catkins, or her. He walked back to
the Manor House with her, and drew her into conversation that day; but on subsequent evenings, when he
came in to chat half-an-hour with old Mr. Serle,
Sydney found herself as far from feeling at ease in
his presence as ever. She persevered in keeping aloof
from the rest of the party, and sat silent in her
window recess, sewing diligently, while he was delight-
ing the others with his pleasant talk, and when he
turned round suddenly to address a remark to her, as
happened now and then, she was generally too much
startled to do more than acknowledge it with the same
sort of half-murmured assent, that Mr. Humphreys had to
put up with in exchange for his botanical maxims. When
he had gone, and the door had closed behind him, she
could hardly bear her anger against herself for having lost
so much, and behaved so stupidly; yet she was sure to
act precisely in the same manner the next time he came.

Colonel Edgecombe, however, was by no means disposed to quarrel with her shy silence; the sudden uplifting of her large, childish, admiring, brown eyes to his face, was quite as much answer as he thought necessary. There was already rather more loud talking in the old Manor House parlour than suited with the peaceful dreamy recollection he had so long kept in his mind. He was glad that there was still old Mr. Serle's benevolent placid face, and Sydney's quiet figure, enclosed in the setting of the old window-frame, through which straggling branches of sweetbriar peeped in, to justify his old notions of the picturesqueness of the place. If Sydney had been mixed up with Mrs. George and the noisy children, she would have belonged to the disenchanting present of Manor Combe; as it was, her silence gave her the distinction of harmonising with pleasant memories of the past.

Moreover, Colonel Edgecombe had no wish to be better acquainted with Sydney Serle. It was all very well to have a pretty picture in his mind of the drooping, graceful figure shrined in the old window recess, and of the reverentially admiring eyes timidly turned towards him; but it would have perplexed and disturbed him very much just then if this vision had come to hold too prominent a place in his thoughts. He had returned from India at a great sacrifice of his own inclination, mainly with the object of atoning to his mother for the unhappiness he had caused her ten years before, when impatience under the discomforts of home had driven him to escape from Combe, and abandon her to bear her sorrows as best she could alone. He had felt at times a good deal of uncomfortable remorse for having deserted his mother just as he arrived at an age when she might have looked to him for support, and he resolved to wipe out old scores and reinstate himself for ever in his own good opinion by this signal act of self-sacrifice performed for her sake. He had had no pleasant anticipation of what life at High Combe with his mother would be, and it was a great relief to him when he was settled there to find that he could accommodate himself to his new circumstances, and put aside the interests and ambitions that had hitherto occupied him wholly, with less pain than he had expected. The discovery filled him with satisfaction and universal benevolence to every one : he resolved more firmly than ever to devote himself to his mother, and make her life so happy that all remembrance of past trials would be obliterated from her mind for ever.

He had not been at home a week before he discovered the plan for his future, on which she had so vehemently set her heart. He was merely lazily amused at first. He could not bear to ruffle the harmony between them by the least show of opposition; he would leave it to circumstances and the quiet course of time to show her there were limits to her power of determining his destiny. By the end of the first month he was more than willing to let the smoothly-flowing current of events drift him to the goal she had foreseen. He had discovered by that time, that there might be some difficulty in finding a new mistress of High Combe, with whom the old mistress could live happily; and as he had determined long ago that his home and his mother's must always be the same, it seemed a crowning mark of good fortune that the one young girl who did perfectly please her, should also be the very one whom he should have chosen for his wife, if he had been quite left to himself. He took a great deal of pains to convince himself of this fact; and when he was alone in the evenings, or on his solitary ride, he was constantly thinking over Clemency's perfections, and making a catalogue of them in his mind. Could he possibly have made a better choice if he had searched the world over? How perfect her beauty was, and her mind was as superior to other people's as her face. In all the frank revelations she had made of her thoughts and feelings during their many hours of close intercourse, he reflected that she had never said a word that did not perfectly meet his approbation and satisfy his taste.

His mother had shown wonderful discernment in the choice she had made. Any one might be proud to win such a wife—and yet—and yet—saying all this a thousand times, and fully believing that he was very much in love, it had still somehow or other to be said again and held up consciously before his eyes, that he might see and feel it. If only his mother had not planned this marriage for him, or at least had not let him see so plainly that her happiness depended on his compliance with her wish. Again and again, do what he would, his thoughts returned to this point. The air of Combe had always been poisoned by a galling sense of restraint that seemed to come over him whenever he breathed it. In former times it was his father's innumerable petty restrictions and exactions that made life there a wearisome bondage ; but now, he sometimes asked himself, was not the claim his mother, in her absorbing love, made to absolute disposal of his heart and purpose, more enslaving still. He wished very much that she had been less eager and impetuous in planning happiness for him, even at the moment when he was most thoroughly convinced that nothing would make him so happy as the success of her plan.

He was not romantic, but he had had his dreams, and it did not quite please him that the great event of his life should come so easily, so openly, with so little mystery and emotion about it; he had always expected that some time or other he should experience a great deal and be very much moved out of his usual course. If he had felt any great anxiety about his chance of winning Clemency, these minor objections would have been forgotten or swallowed up; but he believed her too entirely devoted to his mother to have any choice or wish of her own. He did not flatter himself that he had any hold on her heart; he thought she would accept the lot arranged for her, when she was made aware of it, as easily, as naturally, as prosaically, as he had resolved to do. He did not imagine Clemency to be a person of very deep feeling; she seemed to him to have too many interests and too much general benevolence to be capable of that entire absorbing devotion to one person which he considered the most lovable quality in a woman. Her extreme frankness and unconsciousness troubled him, too, sometimes. The clear blue eyes, in which one might almost see the eager thoughts and questions floating up before the lips began to speak

them, were a little too easy to read he thought; there
was no depth or mystery in them; they were always
equally clear, and frank, and kind. He could fancy a
look in shy eyes that would interest him more.

But these were after all only occasional misgivings,
that came when he was tired of contemplating his good
fortune. When he was next in his mother's and Clemency's company he was sure to be disgusted with himself for having ever entertained them. He looked into
the blue eyes he had presumed to criticise, listened to
the pleasant frank talk, grave or gay, and perhaps
allowed a sense of past injustice to give a shade more
affectionate deference to his manner, than would have
been there, if he had had no previous disparaging
thoughts to atone for.

So circumstanced, and in such a state of mind, it
would have been extremely provoking and disturbing
to him if the Manor Combe parlour, with Sydney sitting
in the window, had come to have any attraction that
did not depend on old memories. He did not confess
to himself that he had any fear of such a catastrophe.
Sydney was wrong in thinking he avoided her consciously, he was merely passively content that nothing
should happen to make them better acquainted with
each other; and when after a time one or two slight

circumstances so fell out as to throw them together, he had no ready-made resolution to put him on his guard against them. When two people have been secretly a good deal occupied with each other in their thoughts, a very slight opening will suffice to make a sudden intimacy spring up between them. They don't understand how it is that they seem to know each other so well all at once, and the surprise of the discovery disposes them to make more of the apparent mutual understanding than it is worth.

Mrs. George Serle's obstinacy about not having fires lighted in the sitting-room, after the established day for leaving off fires had passed, was the first link in the chain of events that brought Sydney and Colonel Edgecombe into closer communication with each other.

Old Mr. Serle and George were always driven by the chill discomfort of the Manor Combe drawing-room on a rainy spring or summer evening to take refuge in the warm kitchen. The children, weary with a whole day of in-door amusements, were sure to be sent off early to bed. Mrs. George made unfavourable weather an excuse for extra activity in the house; and so it happened, that when one wet evening Colonel Edgecombe walked over from High Combe to congratulate old Mr. Serle on the rain, for want of which he had been sighing,

he for the first time found no one in the sitting-room
to receive him but Sydney.

He had let himself in at the front door, and walked
unceremoniously into the parlour as he was accustomed to do, and for a minute or two he thought
there was no one there. Sydney did not hear him
enter; she was in her usual place in the window
seat, but she was not sewing, and there was no sign
of employment near her or about the room, which
wore that chill, over-tidy aspect considered by Mrs.
George proper to rooms except at meal times. She
was looking listlessly out of the window at the great
drops of rain as they trickled from leaf to leaf of the
trellised rose-tree and fell with a plash on the gravel
walk below. In her whole figure, from the little hand
on the window-frame, against which she was leaning
her cheek, to the pose of the small foot that touched
the floor, there was an expression of extreme weariness
and dejection that struck Colonel Edgecombe quite
painfully when, on coming further into the room, his
eye fell upon her. What could such a little thing as
that have to grieve about, he wondered: who could
have been vexing her? He did not think of any serious
sorrow, only of some passing, easily dispelled trouble,
such as one might pity a child for; and he thought

how pleasant it would be to be able to send it away and to see the dejected figure grow alert and the childish eyes brighten again. He spoke before he came close to the window, and Sydney gave such a start, and made such haste to pass her hand over her eyes and cheeks, that it was quite clear to him there had been other drops falling besides those from the rose leaves outside.

It was rather difficult to begin an easy conversation under such circumstances, and he felt relieved when his eye fell on a branch of double-blossomed cherry that lay on the window-seat, as it gave him something to remark upon.

"How beautiful!" he said, lifting it up; "but how heavy with wet the blossoms are. Some one must have been out in the rain to gather it."

"Yes, papa brought it in just now; he thinks a great deal of that tree. Mrs. Edgecombe brought it when it was a little slip from High Combe, and planted it in our orchard on my christening-day. It was meant to be a real cherry-tree—a fruit-tree, I mean—but there was some mistake about it. Papa never will allow he is sorry. He brought that branch in just now because he said as there never was to be anything but blossoms he would not have them all beaten down by the rain."

" Quite right too, one cannot take too much care of such fragile, beautiful things. I think my mother made a clever mistake. But where is the tree? I wonder I never noticed it."

"Just in the middle of the orchard. You would not be likely to see it, for it has only just come into flower. Lizzie (my sister-in-law) says it is a shame that such a worthless tree should have the sunniest place in the orchard. She has just been advising George to cut it down, and she said at the same time—that I——"

Here the tearful note in Sydney's voice was so perceptible that Colonel Edgecombe interposed quickly.

" You must not tell me that your sister has been making comparisons between you and your tree. I can't give her credit for so much imagination, or for saying anything so much to the purpose."

" To the purpose ! Oh, but I don't like it at all. How would you like to be told twenty times a-day that you were of no more use than a fruitless cherry-tree, and could you bear to be made to feel that your place in the house was grudged you, as well as the tree's place in the orchard ? "

Sydney spoke feelingly, and her large tear-filled eyes had an appealing, injured expression in them which, to Colonel Edgecombe's imagination, told a whole romance of unappreciated sweetness, and intelligence thrown away. He could hardly keep down his indignation to answer as lightly as he wished.

"I am afraid I should not care for the accusation much. I have outlived all remorse for being useless ; I have not the intense respect for activity the good people about here seem to have. Can't you be content to be useless in the same way these are ?" (holding up the rain-wet blossoms.) "Why should fruit to eat be better than flowers to admire and delight in ? To be sure, there will always be people like your sister-in-law, who can only appreciate the obvious coarse use; but you must not mind them. Let them be active in their own common-place way, and look down on the flowers and you. They are not all the world."

There was a good deal in this speech that Sydney did not comprehend ; but she gathered that Colonel Edgecombe classed her with himself, and preferred her to Lizzie, and there was untold balm in the discovery. The sorrowful lines went out of her face, the ready tears welled back to their source, and the change in attitude and expression, which Colonel Edgecombe had thought he should like to see, came all at once.

"What a sweet little April face it is," he thought. "What a gentle, tender, impressionable nature. My

mother has made a great mistake in not doing more
for one so evidently misunderstood by the common-
place people about her."

"I wish you would say just what you have been saying to me, to Lizzie," Sydney remarked, looking up
shyly, after a minute's pause. "She would believe it if
you said it, for she thinks a great deal of you; but she
only laughs at papa and me. She would treat us differently if she thought you were on our side."

"Indeed! I am much obliged by her good opinion;
but I had no idea that your sister was such a formidable person. I shall begin to weigh my words, for I
should be very sorry to speak on the wrong side. What
other useless things am I to uphold Mr. Serle in
valuing, besides double-blossomed cherry trees and—
you?"

"Oh, a great many," Sydney began, gravely, not
quite understanding the playful smile that accompanied
the last half of the sentence, but feeling all its kindness. "I could tell you of a great many things that
papa likes, and that Lizzie sets her face against so
contemptuously. But she is coming in. She will be
very angry if she thinks we have been talking about
her."

"She shall not think so. I shall trust to you to

enlighten me further on your father's tastes at the next favourable opportunity. Mind you do."

And as the door opened Colonel Edgecombe went forward to meet Mrs. George, with the branch of cherry still in his hand. During the conversation that followed he contrived to bring in so many allusions to its beauties that Sydney, in her far seat by the window, could hardly keep her amused, delighted smile from degenerating into a quite audible titter.

"Have I managed well?" he asked Sydney, in a low voice, as he wished her good-night last of the party; and it did not escape her observation that he carried the cherry branch away with him, though its blossoms, from having been battered by the rain, were beginning to droop already.

The rain had ceased when Colonel Edgecombe took leave, and he walked rather slowly home through the wood, enjoying the fragrant smell of the rain-refreshed ground and the sound of the plash of heavy drops falling from the wet trees. He was a great lover of Nature, in a somewhat unobserving sort of way. It influenced his moods rather than his thoughts; the aspect without, though he took little conscious note of it, entered into him and swayed the whole tone of his mind into harmony with it.

The tender grey sky and dim green earth, on such
an evening as this, had a quieting effect, making him
in love with repose and stillness.

"How very much over-exertion and effort there is in
our lives," he reflected, as he walked along. "We cultivated people are all too full of thought and restless
striving after intellectuality in these days. It becomes
infinitely wearisome. How much more interest there
is, after all, in a simple character, where natural feeling has been more developed than thought. My dear
mother has the one drawback of being a little over-
cultivated. No one who is much with her can ever
have a mind at rest. It is like living always in full
sunlight. Now, I must say I like a little dim shade
like this sometimes."

Reaching home brought a sudden check to his
thoughts. He stood still for a minute at the bottom of
the steps leading to the conservatory, as if he were almost
surprised to find himself there, and before he entered he
tossed the branch of cherry blossom he had been carrying hastily away. He found his mother in the drawing-
room, with a large book on her knee, and a case of
bronzes he had brought from India on a table before
her. She called to him eagerly, as he entered:—

"I have made them all out, Walter. This is precisely

the book we want. We shall get on with our catalogue
famously now. How clever it was of Clemency to remember this book ; and, see, she has put marks in the
pages where the information we want is to be found.
One would think she had studied Indian antiquities all
her life, instead of the one month since I asked her to
help with our catalogue. She has a very pleasant way
of throwing herself, heart and soul, into what her friends
are occupied about. It is just what I like."

"And just what is bad for you, my dear mother," he
answered. "I am sure you don't require any spurring.
Your mind is active enough in itself, and does not want
urging on by Miss Franklyn. One may have too much
of the best of things."

She looked up, surprised, and saw a little shade of
annoyance on her son's brow. Yet she could not let
the subject drop. She was too overwhelmingly anxious
to know what was passing in his mind to refrain
from probing it. She drew him into an argument
about the indispensability of intellectual sympathy to
love and friendship ; and they carried it on till both
were so irritated that, for the first time in their lives,
they were on the verge of saying harsh things to each
other.

CHAPTER X.

An inventive Age
Has wrought, if not with speed of magic, yet
To most strange issues.   *   *   *   *
The footpath faintly marked, the horse-track wild,
And formidable length of plashy lane,
Have vanished—swallowed up by stately roads,
Easy and bold, that penetrate the gloom
Of Britain's farthest glens.

Wordsworth.

WHEN events do occur in very quiet lives, they almost always come in clusters. Sydney would have made an event of her conversation with Colonel Edgecombe, if the occurrences of the following days had not been too engrossing to leave her leisure to dwell upon it. There had been a cloud of domestic trouble and anxiety hanging over the Manor Combe household for some months, and during the next week the long expected storm burst upon them. The crisis of their difficulties was caused by old Mr. Yonge's sudden determination to exact the payment of a considerable sum of money, which he had lent the Serle's at the time of George's marriage, when old Mr. Serle, with much pain, had consented to mortgage a portion of his estate, to raise money for the payment of his son's debts. It had been a misery and a grievance to him ever since, whenever he thought of it, that is to say, whenever the times for paying the half-yearly interest came round, or when, as happened now and then, he received an incoherent letter from Mr. Yonge, requiring speedy payment of the principal.

Many of these letters had come lately, and been put aside. Mr. Serle was very much annoyed for an hour or so after reading them; but Mr. Yonge's oddity was so well known, and he had so often before written without taking any further steps to execute his threats, that Mr. Serle had not much difficulty in putting the matter out of his mind when his hour's fret was over. An interview, face to face, with a determined creditor, was not so easily forgotten ; and the morning after Colonel Edgecombe's visit, the Serle family was startled by the appearance of Mr. Yonge himself at the Manor House.

It was years since he had been so far from home, and the servant who opened the door for him had some hesitation about letting him in, he presented so strange an appearance, with his long white hair falling forlornly about his face, his preternaturally bright eyes, and dress that had not changed its fashion for twenty years. He would have had to return as he came, if Sydney had not overheard his anxious inquiries for her father, and come forward to bring him into the parlour. She wished many times during the day that she had not happened to pass through the hall just then, or had not interfered, for Mr. Serle was made very unhappy by the interview that followed.

He could put aside and forget importunate letters, but he could not so easily withstand poor old Mr. Yonge's eager entreaties and tremulous remonstrances. He was wrought upon, while Mr. Yonge stayed with him, to promise whatever he thought would send him away most tranquil; and then, when the excitement of the interview was past, the recollection of what his promise involved came over him. The long dreaded trial of having to sell some of his beloved fields must, he saw, come upon him now, and his misery at parting with them was aggravated by foreseeing the destruction to the beauty of the whole valley that might come if they fell into the hands of anyone less set on preserving its seclusion than he was. Every now and then a new project for re-opening the Vale Combe mines was set on foot by some sanguine speculator, and Mr. Serle had to endure rumours about the new road through Vale Combe that would be wanted, and to listen to calculations respecting the vast sums he might expect to raise by selling off his least profitable fields. He lived in dread of such talk reaching Lizzie's ears. He knew that if her cupidity were once roused, she would never let him rest till he had promised not to stand in the way of her dreams of wealth being realised, should the occasion offer; yet the very thought of living to see tall chimneys belching out smoke over Combe Woods, and the little rivulet choked with coal dust, was a torture to him.

What had hitherto been but a distant possibility had within the last month changed into a near prospect. Young Mr. Wilson had actually undertaken to work the mines again, and he had sounded Mr. Serle as to his disposition to allow the new road to pass through his property, and offered him a sum of money for a piece of ground adjoining the mine, which would have paid off his debt to Mr. Yonge twice over. Old Mr. Serle had been extremely thankful at the time the proposition was made that he chanced to be alone when Mr. Wilson spoke to him, and that neither his son George, nor Lizzie were ever likely to know what answer he made. He knew that Lizzie's indignation against him would know no bounds if she ever discovered that he had turned away from an advantageous bargain just to avoid seeing a smelting-house rise at the entrance of the valley, and to prevent trains of coal and ironstone trucks passing up and down his fields. There was nothing Mr. Serle was more firmly resolved on than that Mrs. George should never know what had passed between himself and young Wilson; and yet while he was lamenting over the difficulty of raising the money for Mr. Yonge, he unconsciously betrayed that he had something on his mind of which the rest of the family were ignorant, and could not defend himself from having the whole truth drawn from him by Mrs. George's pertinacious questions. Then the long-dreaded domestic storm broke.

Mr. Serle was too unhappy, and too conscious that he must yield in the end, to make a great show of resistance; but as it was a rainy day, and there was nothing particular to be done outside the house or in, Mrs. George did not allow his passivity to prevent her—as she said, for *once*—speaking out all that was in her mind. It was not enough for her that the poor old man should be brought at last to consent to sacrifice his own feelings, and bring a daily annoyance on himself for the sake of enriching his family. The atrocity of his ever having hesitated to do so; of his so flying in the

face of Providence as not to be thankful for the opportunity of so sacrificing himself, furnished her with a
topic on which she descanted eloquently through all the
dripping, disconsolate hours of that weary day. A con-
tentious woman is a continual dropping, Solomon
says. Mr. Serle did not chance to remember the pro-
verb, but if he had, the regular heavy weeping of the
rose leaves without, and the continuous flow of Mrs.
George's hard words descending upon him within,
would certainly have made him admire the aptness
of the comparison. Sydney did not on that day
attempt to take part in the discussion. She would not
have had any influence, one way or another, if she had,
yet it was unlike her to witness a war of words
between her father and sister-in-law, without making
rash, ill-judged sallies, every now and then, in his
defence. She wandered about the house, and in and
out of the sitting-room, like a person in a dream that
morning, more silent than she had ever been for so long
a time together in her life before. She was not indifferent to what was going on, but her mind was preoccupied by a very strong wish, and a half-formed
purpose, which had flashed upon her the instant the
contention began.

"If Colonel Edgecombe would but call this morning,"

she said to herself, "I would be courageous enough to tell him what has happened. I know he would take papa's part, and perhaps find some way of helping him." With this thought in her mind, she marched restlessly from window to window, half expecting to see the wished-for visitor making his way to them through the rain. He had come once in the rain, why not again? Yet repeated disappointments had made the hope look very dim long before the day or Lizzie's scolding was over. Late in the afternoon, when her eyes quite ached with looking towards the wood path, a new idea presented itself to her mind. Colonel Edgecombe could not guess how much good he could do by walking down to the Manor House, unless some one told him. Why should she not write a line to say that her father wished to see him that evening? Sydney felt that this daring project was one that would not bear much thinking about, and she was glad to remember, at the same time, that it must be executed at once if it was to be done at all. The farm servant who posted the letters at High Combe on his road home, left work early on rainy days. If she wrote at once, she could intrust her note to him, and feel sure that it would be delivered safely, and in time for Colonel Edgecombe to come that evening. Sydney was not much in the habit of writing notes to anyone, and when she did they were usually very carefully concocted and stiffly written missives. A wish to make this one as little like a note as possible, so that the presumption of having written it might be more easily explained away in her own conscience, afterwards impelled her to seize the first scrap of paper that came, and scribble hurriedly in pencil :—

" Please could you come to Manor Combe to-night at eight o'clock. My father is very unhappy, and wants to speak to you. He will be alone in the drawing-room, after tea. You said last night that you would be glad to help him : that was about a little thing—this is a great one, or we would not trouble you."

She did not even read the note over after it was written. She folded it and rushed downstairs to wait for her messenger, panting and breathless, like a child who looks at the sea into which he is going to be plunged. During the five minutes she had to wait in the kitchen, and while she instructed her messenger, and watched him plodding down the road, with his tools and the letter-bag over his shoulder, and her little note hidden in his great hand, the excitement that had worked her up to the step she had taken lasted ; when she turned back into the house, the reaction of doubt and fear began.

But she was used to such alternations of hasty resolve and chill fear : her rash, timid, inconsequent nature was always impelling her in great things or small, to some sudden word or deed that had to be remembered with all manner of misgivings and tremblings of heart afterwards. She was used to suffer these, and to wait passively for such result of her hasty doings as time might bring her. It comforted her much that day to know she should not have to wait long. It was five o'clock when the note was despatched; the three hours till eight must be fretted away in a misery of suspense and wonder at her own daring, but when once Colonel Edgecombe had entered the house, she felt sure that her anxiety would be over. She could not imagine any look on his face that would make her regret having appealed to him, or suppose that any difficulty could arise with which he would not know how to deal.

"You will tell Colonel Edgecombe all that has happened if he should call this evening—won't you, father ?" she said, stopping Mr. Serle on the stairs as he was coming down to tea, to have a moment's talk apart with him.

"But he won't come," Mr. Serle answered, despondingly ; "and if he did, what good could he do me, child?

No, no; best keep one's troubles and one's family quarrels to oneself. I've lived long enough to learn that, if you have not. Colonel Edgecombe will see the change in the valley by-and-by, and perhaps blame me for giving way; but I shall never tell him how I was driven to it."

Poor Sydney's face fell to a degree that would have led a more suspicious person than her father to question her. Yet on reflection she was not altogether discouraged. Mr. Serle might have lived long enough to learn that it was best not to talk of family disagreements, but he had not begun yet to practice the lesson. Sydney knew perfectly that it would be impossible for him to sit an hour with Colonel Edgecombe, or any other person willing to listen, without pouring forth the history of his grievances. After tea she brought her father's writing-desk into the drawing-room, and persuaded him to begin the letter to Mr. Wilson, which Lizzie had exacted should be written that day, quite sure that it would not be nearly finished when the desired interruption came. Then she sat in the window and waited. The sky cleared after sunset as it had done the evening before; the rose-leaves left off weeping; one or two birds found courage to celebrate even-song in the garden—it was a mild, still evening, pleasant enough to tempt anyone to stroll out. Surely he would come. Sydney would hardly let herself believe that the twilight was deepening, and that the hour she had named had passed. Her heart sunk very low, and an overpowering regret for what she had done came over her as the conviction grew. About nine her father called on her to read and fold his letter. She lingered over the reading as long as she could, and while she was still occupied with it, she heard the sound of horse-hoofs coming up the drive. Her heart bounded with joyful expectation and relief, and then the room-door opened—and Mr. Humphreys entered, looking more than usually self-satisfied, and secure of a hearty welcome, since he had been prevented from calling for three whole days.

Sydney was apt to be unreasonably disappointed for very slight causes, but she had never before experienced such a complete revulsion of feeling as came over her then. She had sufficient self-command to shake hands as usual, and answer the common-place remarks about weather and health, which Mr. Humphreys usually distributed scrupulously to every person in the company; but that was all her fortitude could sustain.

When her father drew Mr. Humphreys into conversation, and began, as Sydney had foreseen, to open out on the great event of the day, she could not keep the tears from gathering in her eyes, and falling slowly down on to her work. It *did* seem such a cruel mockery of what she had hoped, such a bitter disappointment. She dare not get up and leave the room, for she knew her father would call her back to ask why she went: she could only hope that both he and Mr. Humphreys were too much occupied to observe her tears.

Neither had she the comfort of finding, as the conversation went on, that her father was gaining anything by his over-communicativeness. Mr. Humphreys was evidently pleased at being consulted, but he had too clear a head for business, and prided himself too much on his strong practical sense, to be induced to see the matter for a moment from old Mr. Serle's point of view. It was very plain to him, that Mr. Serle could not do better than sell those two meadows at the end of the valley, which had always been more productive of rushes and marsh-lilies, than of wholesome grass, to Mr. Wilson, at the price he had named ; and not even the sight of Sydney's tears, every one of which he noted with a little prick of pain, could induce him to say otherwise. When Mr. Serle had done talking, he set himself to put what he considered the rights of the case, forcibly before him, and continued to say so many uncomfortable true things, that if the poor old gentleman had not shed all his tears long ago, he would have been very much disposed to imitate Sydney. Mr. Humphreys had not the smallest notion that he was giving pain to anyone. He thought he was cleverly reconciling his puzzle-headed old friend to the performance of a necessary duty, and made no doubt that he was feeling quite thankful to him for his plain dealing.

When he got up to go, and Mrs. George thanked him for having given her father such excellent advice, and hoped, with a glance at Sydney, that they should all profit by it, he grew quite elated, and declared he did not know how to be thankful enough that he had chanced to drop in so opportunely that evening. He only wished such happy occasions for making himself useful to the family, came oftener. If Miss Sydney, for example, were not quite convinced, it would make him so happy to go over the matter again with her at any convenient time, and do his best to reconcile her to the step her father had taken, and to her good sister's opinion.

The glance he got from under Sydney's swollen eyelids when he came up to shake hands with her after this speech, disturbed his complacency somewhat, and recurred to him unpleasantly during his ride home, as he was thinking over the arguments he had used. He had not known before that those soft, velvet-brown eyes of hers could shoot such dark fire from under their silken lashes.

It would not be pleasant, he confessed, to have such looks from his wife every time he and she chanced to differ in a matter of opinion—but then, it was after all so amiable in Sydney to feel her father's trouble as deeply as she did, so natural that she should be unable to adopt any opinion but his. When she was once married, she would take her husband's views for granted, as she now took her father's; and since no occasions of difference between them could arise, all would be well. With a sensible husband to influence and guide her, as her foolish father was incapable of doing, she would never again have cause to shed such tears as had made her eyelids heavy that night, and his heart sore in spite of all his sense and resolution.

The next day was one of the longest Sydney had ever known. Again there was no going out, and a second unsettled day is always worse than the first. She had her great unhappiness all to herself, too. Her father was calmer. He had sent his letter to Mr. Wilson, and a sense of rest came over him now that the sacrifice he had long been dreading was actually made ; while Mrs. George, having gained her point, was disposed to be almost good-humoured with everyone. Sydney felt very lonely in her self-reproach and anxiety, yet there was no one in the world to whom she dare confess what she had done. If her measure had succeeded, she would not have troubled herself much about the right or wrong of taking it ; since it had failed, she worked herself up into an exaggerated state of self-condemnation. Every moment she expected that Mrs. Edgecombe would arrive at the Manor, to reproach her for taking such a liberty as to write to her son. She imagined all manner of insulting speeches addressed to her by them both, and saw herself overwhelmed with their scorn and anger. Her father could not understand her melancholy, and depressed her still further by sad little expostulations against grieving so over his trouble.

" I ought not to mind it so much. You see, darling," he kept saying ; " it's only a few years—perhaps a few months—sooner. They'd have done it after I was gone. It's only ruining the dear old place a little sooner. There was a good deal of truth in what Mr. Humphreys said, and it was natural he should think of your interest first. I don't blame him in the least for that."

"I do. I hate him!" Sydney cried, impetuously, almost beside herself with pain.

"Hush, darling, hush ; that will never do," Mr. Serle said, stroking her hair as his wont was ; but with such a trembling hand, that Sydney could feel the fluttering of the fingers. "There, darling, we won't talk any more to-day ; I can't have you quarrel with good friends on my account."

He knew very well that his daughter-in-law's mind was set on a marriage between Mr. Humphreys and Sydney ; he had learned to think it might be a good thing himself, and the fear of any new subject of dispute arising among them all, was quite too much for him that day.

In the evening, Sydney made no effort to keep her father in the drawing-room ; but directly after tea she put on her bonnet and set out through the rain on an errand to the village. She meant it to occupy her till long after eight o'clock, but somehow it did not. She could not feel so very unhappy while she was out. More reasonable thoughts came with the fresh air. Possible explanations of Colonel Edgecombe's failure to comply with her request, suggested themselves, and she began to have a hope of finding him at Manor Combe when she returned. Unconsciously she quickened her pace; yet when, on coming in sight of the garden-gate, she perceived Colonel Edgecombe leaning over it in his usual lounging attitude, as if nothing had happened, and no one had waited for him, she felt such a sudden glow of resentment against him for having caused her so much anxiety, that she could not bring herself to speak to him when he opened the gate for her and held out his hand. They walked down the gravelled road side by side in silence for a few minutes; then some heavy drops of rain began to fall; he took her umbrella from her hand to hold it over her. She looked up, and their eyes met; hers full of childish resentment, his surprised and kind.

"I have come at your request, though late," he said, gently. "I hope your father will be able to see me to-night. I shall be so glad if I can be of any use to him."

"It is too late now; there is no use in your coming now," she said, shaking her head.

"Pray don't say so; you will make me so very unhappy. I really could not come last night; we had friends with us, whom I could not leave my mother to entertain alone. Cannot you persuade your father to see me to-night?"

"He will see you; but it is too late. Indeed you cannot help him now; the harm is done."

"And can be undone or remedied. Come, you must trust me. I don't believe in too late. I say it shall not be too late, and you will find I am right. If I thought I had really lost an opportunity of serving your father, I should not forgive myself; but I can't have it so."

The confident, cheerful tones lifted a load from Sydney's spirits.

"Oh! if you could help papa, how glad I should be," she said, with eyes sparkling and cheeks glowing with renewed hope.

"I will," he answered, emphatically; and it was not till the words were spoken, that he perceived the imprudence of giving a distinct promise, without in the least knowing to what embarrassing implication in the Serle family affairs it might lead him.

They had reached the house by this time, and Sydney, having taken Colonel Edgecombe into the drawing-room, and sent her father to join him there, ran up into her own room, where she stayed for nearly an hour, with her elbows resting on the window-sill, and her chin between her hands, thinking, or rather trying to still the too rapid beating of her heart. She did not know whether she were very happy or only very much frightened. Colonel Edgecombe's confident way

of speaking, if it had reassured her, had awed her a
little too. It seemed to increase the responsibility of
the step she had taken. If he could effect so much,
what would her sister-in-law say to her, if she ever
discovered that she had called in his aid? " I have
come at *your* request," he had said. It was somewhat dreadful having it put in that light; and yet
she thought she rather liked it. When it was very
nearly dark, she grew tired of being alone, and went
down-stairs, hoping to glide into the sitting-room, where
all the family were now assembled, without exciting
notice.

Colonel Edgecombe had risen to take leave when she
entered. Old Mr. Serle was shaking him warmly by
the hand, and Sydney heard that some meeting for the
next morning was being arranged.

"I shall have seen young Wilson by that time,"
Colonel Edgecombe was saying; "he is a great friend
of mine, and under obligations to me. When he knows
that I have a particular reason for wishing to purchase
the land we have been speaking about, he will relinquish
his prior claim in my favour. A road through Vale
Combe would be a terrible annoyance indeed; there
would never be any game in the Combe woods again.
We landlords must stand by each other to prevent it.

You have done a most neighbourly act in consulting me."

When he wished Sydney good-night, his eyes were dancing with amusement and triumph.

"There, you see," he half whispered, "it is all right; and I have only to thank you for letting me know."

"I was so afraid you might be angry," Sydney could not help saying.

"Angry! It was the only sensible thing that seems to have been done in the business. I begin to think that you are the useful person in the house, and that the double-blossomed cherry-tree emblem is a mistake. Good-night; and remember that, seriously, I am very much obliged to you."

The remaining days of that week were the happiest of Sydney's life. Colonel Edgecombe was not a person to do things by halves. Having once interested himself in the Serles' affairs, and been taken into the old man's confidence, he could not rest till he had discovered the best way of relieving him from all the difficulties with which years of mismanagement had surrounded him. He spent a great part of each day either walking over the fields with George, planning improvements which should not clash with old Mr. Serle's prejudices; or shut up in the study, trying, with

Sydney's help, to extract some sort of meaning from his strangely kept accounts and farm journals.

Sydney found herself in greater request than she had ever been before in her life. From being a nonentity, she had suddenly become the mainspring of the household. Her father and brother showed her more affection than they had dared to do of late years; Lizzie ceased to interfere with her; and Colonel Edgecombe seemed to consider that nothing could be properly done without her co-operation.

A stronger head than hers might have been turned by all this homage; and that no rude shock might come to shatter her content, it chanced that Mr. Humphreys was so much occupied with illness among his patients at Tunstall, that he could not, during the whole week, spare an hour for a visit to Manor Combe. When his name chanced to be mentioned by one of the children one evening, it sounded to Sydney almost like a long-forgotten word. The times when he used to sit by the window and talk to her, as Colonel Edgecombe was doing then, seemed already very far away. She had surely entered another life since then; the thought of going back to the old, made her shudder.

CHAPTER XI.

" Friends—lovers that might have been."

Browning.

MRS. FRANKLYN was one of those people who take a kind of pleasure in attributing misfortune to themselves, and speaking as if all events, including the weather, were ordered by some spiteful power for no other end but to thwart and annoy them. "It always rained," Mrs. Franklyn was in the habit of declaring, "when she wanted it to be fine ; and whenever she had taken particular pains to get up an entertainment, some one was sure to be ill, or some public disaster threw a gloom over people's spirits, expressly that *she* might be disappointed and put out." This sensible notion of Providence was confirmed in her mind by numerous *contretemps*, which occurred during her preparation for the ball at the Red House, which was to take place at the end of Clemency's visit. To say nothing of misdemeanors of servants and tradespeople,

who always, by her own account, behaved worse to Mrs.
Franklyn than to anyone else. Aunt Bessie contrived
to be more unwell than usual, and required a great
deal of the time and attention which Clemency would
otherwise have devoted to listening to her step-mother's
schemes and worries. Mr. Franklyn's silent glooom
deepened with every token of preparation that met
his eye; and what was worst of all, rumours reached
the Red House that Colonel Edgecombe thought it
possible he might be summoned to London on business
the very day before Mrs. Franklyn's entertainment.

Mrs. Franklyn's indignation was very great when
this danger was first made known to her. She could
only comfort herself by remarking that such a disappointment would not have happened to anyone else.
Everyone else in the neighbourhood, who had invited
Colonel Edgecombe, had had their entertainments duly
honoured; but she supposed she ought to have learned
by this time not to expect the same consideration that
other people met with.

The persistency with which she dilated on this
grievance was a great annoyance to Clemency during
the whole fortnight of her visit at the Red House.
Her step-mother could not name Colonel Edgecombe
without significant looks at her; nor could she by

any means be persuaded that Clemency could not have given an explanation of Colonel Edgecombe's probable movements if she had chosen. Clemency, who was so intimate at High Combe, must be able to judge whether this talk of business in London were a mere pretext to escape this party or not ; and if so, she, more than anyone else, ought to feel aggrieved, and set herself to discover the reason of such insulting conduct. Mrs. Franklyn said she hated suspicious or huffy people ; but, at the same time, she had no patience with those who were so deficient in proper spirit as never to know when they were slighted. Her anxiety not to be of the number made her unusually prying and alert at this period.

Clemency saw less than usual of the inmates of High Combe while she was at the Red House ; but Colonel Edgecombe called once or twice, and ten days after she left Tunstall there came an invitation from Mrs. Edgecombe to Mrs. Franklyn and herself to spend a day at Combe. Clemency was half disposed to try to dissuade her step-mother from accepting the invitation, for she knew that in Mrs. Franklyn's present irritable state of temper, there was small hope of the visit giving pleasure to anyone. The two short calls Colonel Edgecombe had made at the Red House, had been very uncomfortable times to her. Mrs. Franklyn, on the alert to feel herself slighted, had sat in her stiffest company attitude on the sofa while he stayed, and cross-questioned him about the time of his proposed visit to London, till even his good-humoured tolerance of what he called Tunstall manners was nearly exhausted. Clemency kept in the back-ground and maintained a, strict silence, partly from shame and partly from fear of having every word that passed between her and their visitor repeated and commented upon when he was gone. She saw that her silence and constraint surprised Colonel Edgecombe, and that he did not at all relish being left exclusively to Mrs. Franklyn's entertainment, and she was very sorry; but she knew there was no help for it.

With this experience she would gladly have avoided the risk of spending a long idle day (sometimes an ordeal to the friendship of real friends) with people so predisposed to misunderstand her and each other, as her mother and the Edgecombes just then evidently were; but she found that any show of unwillingness to accompany Mrs. Franklyn to Combe, would have been received as a crowning offence. Though Mrs. Franklyn took twenty-four hours to answer the note, and affected to be surprised at Mrs. Edgecombe's want of consideration in expecting her to give up a whole day when she was known to be so much occupied, Mrs. Franklyn was, in reality, very much elated at being invited to spend a day at High Combe; not that she expected any particular pleasure there, but because very few people in the neighbourhood ever were asked for the day to Combe, and she looked upon the invitation as a certificate of her superiority over her neighbours. She should not enjoy it, but it would be something to talk of afterwards.

It was well that she had some after-prospect to console herself with, for when the day came she found more annoyance to her irritable vanity, and less gratification of any kind than she had expected. With the full glory and stateliness of High Combe actually before her eyes, she could not quite compass the generosity of really wishing Clemency to be lifted up into it, so far above her head; and the conflict of feeling between longing for the distinction of having a relation reigning there, and grudging that that relation should be the step-daughter she had always looked on as a rival, disturbed her so much, and made her so jealous of every attention paid to her daughter instead of to herself, that she could hardly keep up even the semblance of good-humour. Clemency, who knew every turn of her face and was anxious to spare her mortification, kept

out of everyone's way as much as she could, and
longed for the day to be over before she had been in
the house half an hour.

There were other disagreeables, too, which disturbed
Clemency even more than her step-mother's irritability,
because she had not expected them. Mrs. Edgecombe,
though kinder than ever to her, did not look happy;
the cloud between herself and her son which Clemency
hoped had [been dispelled, seemed to have returned
again. All through the day Mrs. Edgecombe watched
her son with a shade of anxiety upon her brow, and
when Clemency referred to any of the occupations they
had all shared during her last visit to Combe, she
evaded the subject as if it would not bear talking
about, or made it an occasion of bringing out a half-
playful, half-complaining remark on her son's excessive
industry, which had put a stop to all the old pleasures.
Colonel Edgecombe did not show any signs of excessive
occupation that day; but though he was in and out of
the drawing-room all the morning, and accompanied
the ladies in their afternoon walk, he never succeeded
in getting more than ten minutes' uninterrupted conversation with Clemency the whole time. Mrs. Franklyn, who was extremely afraid of Mrs. Edgecombe
when she chanced to be in a sarcastic mood, always

contrived to break up the least approach to a tête-à-
tête, and obliged the whole party to keep together, and
Clemency was too much in dread of what her step-mother
might say afterwards, not to fall in with her views.

All day everyone seemed to be at cross purposes ;
and as the hours passed, each one grew more discontented with the conduct of the others. Just as they
were preparing to take leave, Mrs. Edgecombe found an
opportunity of reproaching Clemency privately with her
reserve and silence.

" My dear," she said, " I can't make you out to-day ;
you are not the least in the world like yourself. Did
you make a vow before you came, to stick close to Mrs.
Franklyn's side all day, and not bestow a word on any
one else ? or have I, or has Walter, done anything to
offend you ? "

" Oh, no, no, indeed ! " Clemency answered, quickly.
" It is only—it is Mrs. Franklyn—things she has been
saying to me—Red House worry, and gossip, in short,
that weighs on my mind and makes me so disagreeable.
Please don't ask any more. I can't help it, indeed."

As Clemency finished speaking, a vivid flush came
into her face ; for just at the moment she caught Colonel
Edgecombe's eyes resting reproachfully, enquiringly, on
her, and a recollection of what the gossip had been

about flashed into her mind. She could hardly keep
the tears from her eyes, and she felt completely miserable when, the next moment, Mrs. Franklyn came up
to hurry her to the carriage, which was waiting to take
them home.

Colonel Edgecombe had unfortunately overheard the
conversation, and when he came to think it over afterwards he fancied he quite understood the cause of the
confusion—angry confusion, he considered it—which
had accompanied Clemency's words. It explained to
him the change in her manner, over which he had been
puzzling ever since his first call at the Red House.

As soon as their guests had gone he set out on his
usual evening walk to Manor Combe, and as he strolled
through the wood he thought over the incoherent sentences again till their meaning became perfectly clear
to him. Mrs. Franklyn had no doubt penetrated his
mother's object in throwing him and Clemency so
much together, and had enlightened her daughter on
the construction the Tunstall gossips were putting on
their intimacy; and now Clemency was making this
marked change in her manner, to show him that her
former friendliness had only been the result of circumstances. He told himself emphatically now that he had
always known she did not care for him—that he had

all along interpreted the frank kindness of her manner
rightly. There was no occasion for any change. He
might have been very much disappointed, he thought,
if he had not always understood her; and even as it
was, he could not help feeling angry with his mother,
whose imprudent haste had drawn so much observation
upon them, and exposed him to such an unnecessary
mortification. When he reached Manor Combe he was
in a mood to be more pleased than usual with the
eager gratitude with which he was received there,
and to find that Sydney's pretty timid cordiality and
reverential manner of listening to all he said, made
up for any lack of conversational power he might
have been disposed to complain of in the rest of the
party.

During the next few days he threw himself more
vehemently than ever into the business of arranging
Mr. Serle's affairs. He wanted occupation; and as this
had come opportunely, he gave his attention vigorously
to it, spent as many hours of every day as he could out
of doors, and, when he was in the house, tried hard not
to see his mother's anxious looks, or to be provoked by
the querulous tone of questioning him about his employments into which she had fallen. Yet the estrangement between them, slight as it was, weighed heavily

on his spirits. He could not have borne the thought of its lasting. He put a term to it, in his own mind, by resolving that he would leave Combe for a time, and on his return begin on a new footing, having had an explanation with his mother, which should set her mind at rest, and induce her to be a little less exacting. Meanwhile he found the Vale Combe parlour, even with the drawbacks of Mrs. George and the noisy children, a more agreeable place to rest in, on the evenings of busy days, than the drawing-room at home, with the tokens of the studies and amusements he had shared with Clemency, filling every corner, and his mother's anxious eyes following him about. As long as he felt himself useful, and was wanted at Manor Combe, he managed to have a sort of satisfaction in going there. It might be different by-and-by. What he was doing now, need not be a criterion for future action. A little pause or lull in life, the deeds of which need not determine anything of the future, might surely be allowed now and then.

The prospect of Mrs. Franklyn's ball had been very disagreeable to him since he had perceived his mother's extreme vexation at his intimacy with the Serles. He had resolved to escape the perplexity of spending a whole evening in the same room with them and her, by

leaving Combe a day or two before the party, but a
few words which Sydney let fall one evening made him
change his mind.

He discovered that she was depending on his countenance and support for courage to go among a set
of people whom she fancied looked down upon her,
and that all prospect of the enjoyment to which she
had been looking forward for days, would be dashed if
he were not there, to help her through the evening.
The look of utter dismay that came over Sydney's
face, when she heard him speak of leaving home
before the ball, told more than her words ; and old
Mr. Serle, who had never quite approved of her going
to Mrs. Franklyn's house, began immediately to raise
fresh objections.   She had much better give up the
idea altogether, he said.   He should never have let
her accept the invitation at all if Colonel Edgecombe
had not advised it ; he was sure she would be very
unhappy, and quite out of place among all the fine
people of the county, who had taken to looking down
upon them of late years, though there had been Serles
at Manor Combe quite as long as there had been Edgecombes, and a century before any of these upstart
grandees had ever been heard of.   From this point he
wandered into anecdotes of slights, fancied or real, that

he had received from his rich neighbours; and Colonel Edgecombe grew indignant as he listened, and resolved at all events to do his part in showing the supercilious *nouveaux riches* of Tunstall and Hemsley how the real old aristocracy of the country, however fallen, ought to be esteemed.

He considered that his mother had never quite done her duty in upholding the Manor Combe family in the neighbourhood, and he decided not to lose so good an opportunity as this assembly at Mrs. Franklyn's would afford, of showing how he regarded them. The notion of distinguishing pretty, graceful, little Sydney before all the purse-proud vulgar people, who presumed to look down upon her, was very agreeable to him; and besides, since he had drawn her and her father into an awkward position, he could not possibly desert them in it.

Sydney thought her cup of happiness was quite full when she understood that Colonel Edgecombe had determined to put off his journey for two days, on purpose to save her from the danger of sitting still all the evening at Mrs. Franklyn's ball. That she should really be going to a ball; that her father should be pleased, and her sister-in-law silent about it; and that she should know for certain that she should dance at least one dance, and with Colonel Edgecombe, seemed quite too much pleasure and excitement for her heart to hold. Lizzie was reduced to the last point of exasperation during the next few days by Sydney's restlessly gay humour, her incessant flittings in and out, and up and down the house, for no object whatever but happy love of motion, her little snatches of song, and her encouragement of the children in all manner of extravagant frolics.

Old Mr. Serle basked in his darling's sunshine, and Colonel Edgecombe, while poring with him over maps of the estate and reports of road surveyors, could not help raising his eyes now and then to smile at the rapid exits and entrances of the bright face and dancing figure. He did not find after all that there was anything disturbing to his idea of the old house in Sydney's songs and laughter.

But Sydney's pleasure had still one more crown to receive. On the evening of the day before the ball, while her father and Colonel Edgecombe were as usual busied over some papers in the sitting-room, and she was flitting through the open window in and out of the garden, a parcel was brought directed to her, which had come by rail from London. She ran eagerly to the window-seat to unpack it, followed by a group of open-mouthed children, to whom the unpacking of an unexpected parcel was a matter of deep interest. When the box-lid was raised she uttered a breathless exclamation of admiration, and lifted up a beautiful wreath of double white cherry-blossoms and green leaves.

"How lovely!" she cried. "Oh, papa, how good you are. You knew I was sorry to have nothing to wear on my head, and you have got me this; but it is too beautiful."

Mr. Serle left his papers at the first appearance of the flowers, and hurried to the window-seat, almost as surprised and delighted as his little daughter. He had no idea such beautiful imitations could be made, he said, as he turned the wreath round and round in his hand. Yes, he had heard of Sydney's wish—every one in the house had heard of it; but he could claim no thanks; such a pretty way of gratifying her would never have come into his mind.

Neither Lizzie nor George could throw any light on the mystery; and while the discussion went on, Colonel Edgecombe kept his place at the table, gravely marking a new boundary on the map, and never once turning his head in the direction of the excited group in the window-seat. At last Sydney approached the table with the wreath in her hand, and stood quite a minute opposite him.

" Who can have given me this ?" she said, timidly.

He was obliged to look up, and the expression of the brown eyes that met his surprised him. They were not dancing with childish delight as he had expected to see them; they had an earnestness of thanks in them that he was not prepared for. He hardly knew whether the sudden emotion that glance caused him, was remorse or pain or pleasure; he only knew it was what he had not bargained for; he had meant to enjoy the satisfaction of seeing easily pleased people simply happy; this deep gratitude for such a trifling gift had not come into his plan. It must be put lightly aside, however pleasant it might be.

" Who gave you that ? Your fairy godmother, I should have said, if it had been more worthy of fairyland. It is not much of a gift."

' My godmother—Mrs. Edgecombe ! Do you really mean that she has been so good as to send me this ? How shall I thank her ?"

" You must not thank her ; fairy godmothers don't like to be thanked ; and, besides, it is not worth saying anything about, I think."

He looked resolutely down on the map again, and

Sydney left the room to put her wreath carefully away, her pleasure in it just a little faded. Colonel Edgecombe saw the change, and when he wished her goodnight could not help wishing to call back her smiles again.

"Remember we are to have a very happy evening to-morrow," he said.

"It would be very ungrateful in me if I were not happy," Sydney answered low, this time without looking at him, but with a note of the same earnestness in her voice that had looked out of her eyes before.

It was late when he left the house, and Colonel Edgecombe walked quickly home through the wood, thrusting aside the interposing branches of trailing briar with unnecessary energy as he went. He was working himself up into a self-justifying state of indignation against his mother's prejudices and love of planning. He wished heartily that she had not been living at Combe all these years, and that they could have begun their life together among people with whom she had no previous ties. Then he might have chosen friends for himself, unbound by her unhappily strong likes and dislikes. For the first time he recognised the possibility of these causing a terrible dissension between them. Yet, how easily, he thought, it might have been otherwise. If only

Clemency had been as loving and as easy to please as Sydney. A little more like Sydney, perhaps, in some things, and yet beloved by his mother as much as ever ; how happy they might all have been together ! He saw it all in a sort of vision as he walked. Some one with Sydney's changeful eyes, and timid voice, and playful unexpected ways, loved by his mother as Clemency was loved, understanding her, occupying her, bearing with her, filling the old dull house with intellectual activity and sunshine as he had seen Clemency do. Such a person as that, how he could have loved ! How well with such an one he could have fulfilled the promise he had made to himself of making High Combe a perfectly happy home for his mother for the rest of her days ! How easy and pleasant life would have been to them all, under such circumstances ! It looked very far from being easy and pleasant, when he waked from his idle dreams, on entering the house and was compelled, by some disparaging remark of his mother's respecting the Serles, to realise how utterly unlike his vision, were the actual facts he had to deal with.

Mrs. Edgecombe did not find him an altogether agreeable companion during the rest of the evening, though she exerted herself to converse on subjects that she thought would interest him, knowing it was the last

they should spend together for some time. Her remarks received more and more inattentive impatiently-
spoken replies, till at last a silence crept in between
them—that same brooding, weighty, palpable silence,
that in past times the High Combe sitting-rooms had
known so well. How little, a few months ago, Mrs.
Edgecombe would have believed anyone who had told
her that, in her own home, in her son's presence, she
should ever breathe it again !

CHAPTER XII.

Come back in tears,
O memory, hope, love of finished years.

Christina Rossetti.

Miss Arnays had expressed a wish to see Clemency dressed for her first ball, and Mrs. Edgecombe was so pleased to find her friend capable of taking an interest in such an ordinary mundane proceeding, that she gave herself a good deal of trouble to have the wish gratified. She persuaded Mrs. Franklyn to allow Clemency to leave the Red House a day or two sooner than had been intended, and arranged to convey her to Tunstall on the morning of the party, and to call for her again in the evening on her way to the ball. Mrs. Franklyn liked the appearance of intimacy between the two families, which this arrangement countenanced, and Clemency was heartily rejoiced to change the bustle of the Red House the day before an entertainment, for the quiet of her own home; but Miss Arnays had some scruples about the wisdom of the measure, which the delight of welcoming Clemency back could not quite put aside. Even when Mrs. Edgecombe and Clemency arrived, looking very happy, and assuring her that they had left Mrs. Franklyn in a most gracious mood, she was not quite satisfied.

"It is very good of you both to make so much of me," she said; "but Clemency is Mrs. Franklyn's eldest daughter. Is it right of her to leave the house to-day when there is so much to be done?—and will not her coming to her first ball with you, instead of remaining under her step-mother's charge, strike people as rather odd? It is dividing her from her own family. The arrangement does not quite please me."

"But it quite pleases me, Bessie," Mrs. Edgecombe answered, decidedly; "so don't you, who know nothing of the world, begin to raise objections. This ball would have been a terrible penance to me, if I had been obliged to see Clemency acting as one of the hostesses. I shall be able to bear it tranquilly, when I feel that she is no more responsible than I am myself, for the tasteless display that is sure to spoil everything."

Clemency had left the room before the conversation commenced; but Miss Arnays looked pained and disconcerted by it.

"I am too weak to argue with you," she said; "but one word I must say. Is it really kind of you to make Clemency dissatisfied with her own home?—are you not making life harder to her by teaching her to criticise the people with whom she will have to live—you don't know how soon?"

"Never; that is just what I do know. Fortunately she has not hitherto been mixed up with the Red House society, and *now* would be a foolish time to begin. You must trust me, Bessie. You shall confess some day soon that I have been a judicious friend to Clemency. Sometimes I ask myself if I am not even more anxious about her happiness than about Walter's. If I could have a hand in building it up, how glad I should be. I should look back on the past with less pain, if I could think I had atoned to you for the deep sorrow I once caused you, by helping to make some one you love happy."

Mrs. Edgecombe spoke quickly, and felt sorry for her words, when she saw the look of distress that came over Miss Arnays' face on hearing them. Clemency's entrance interrupted the conversation opportunely, but it was some time before Aunt Bessie recovered her tranquillity, and all day, even when she and Clemency were alone together, she showed a disposition, not at all usual with her, to turn the conversation on the events of past times. Clemency was delighted to hear her reminiscences; nothing else could so effectually have put away from her mind the bustle and worries of the Red House as the glimpse of her own mother, and the home of her early days, with which Aunt Bessie indulged her for the first time that day.

The pictures Miss Arnays drew were all sunny and pleasant in themselves, yet there was every now and then a tone of sadness in her voice as she spoke, especially, Clemency noticed, whenever Mrs. Edge-combe's name came into any of the stories. Sydney St. Erme she had been in those days,—poor dear Sydney, Aunt Bessie called her, with a note of apology in her voice, of which Clemency longed to ask the meaning. In the course of the afternoon, Arthur Yonge came to wheel Aunt Bessie out in a garden-chair, which he had found in an outhouse in his grand-father's garden, and had repaired for her use. It was the first experiment of the chair, and of Arthur as chairman, and it answered so well as to put them all in good spirits. Aunt Bessie enjoyed taking the air, without the fatigue of walking, or the noise of a carriage, and Arthur persuaded her to let him take her further from the town than she had ventured for years. They stood for a long time at the gate, overlooking Vale Combe, and watched the sun flooding the little valley with glorious afternoon light, and then sinking slowly behind its fir-crowned protecting hills.

They all talked more than usual, more eagerly and intimately, and somehow or other, that afternoon always stood out to Clemency as a distinct period in her life, belonging neither to the bright past that lay behind, nor to the troubled future that followed ; a little island of time, raised up above both, and basking in a quiet light, that did not visit her again for many a day.

Her two companions did not seem to be exactly the same as she had always known them before. Her aunt, roused out of her usual abstraction by the recollections of early days she had been calling round her, was freer in speaking out her inmost thoughts, than it was her wont to be, and Arthur entered into conversation on the grave subjects that came up, more understandingly, than Clemency felt herself capable of doing. She could not help looking up sometimes to see if her old playmate had not grown years older, since they last parted three weeks ago. Some alteration had certainly come over him ; she could not quite make up her mind what it was, but she felt she should look up to him more than she had hitherto done, and perhaps abate something of the old brother-and-sister familiarity.

Mrs. Edgecombe did not call till late, and Clemency, who had dressed quickly for fear of keeping her waiting, had time to make tea for her aunt, and allow herself to be admired in her ball dress, to the content of the little household. Miss Arnays could only talk of some ball for which she had helped to dress Clemency's mother and Sydney St. Erme ; and Clemency, who had a question in her mind she had long wished to ask, encouraged her to pursue her reminiscences.

"I know I am not like mamma," she said ; "one day Mrs. Edgecombe was almost angry with some one who pretended to see a likeness. I wondered why. It might be that she did not think me good enough to be considered like mamma. Yet I don't believe it was that."

"No, nor I," Aunt Bessie answered.

"Mrs. Edgecombe loved mamma very much, I suppose ? "

"Everybody loved her, she was so gentle and unoffending."

"Gentle and unoffending ! Very unlike me, certainly. I have always known that it was not for mamma's sake Mrs. Edgecombe liked me. Yet I am quite sure it is not all for my own."

"May it not be for mine?" Aunt Bessie asked, smiling.

"It ought to be, but——Aunt Bessie, I must ask you one question—not about mamma or me ; one that I have had a long time in my mind ready to ask. Why did Mrs. Edgecombe marry her husband?"

"What a question! Why do persons marry generally?"

"From love and choice, I suppose, and that is what puzzles me, for I never can believe it was so with Mrs. Edgecombe ; how can one, recollecting what he was ? Such a contrast as there was between them."

"The contrast was not always so great. Poor Mr. Edgecombe had not always been what uncontrolled temper and other bad habits made him when you knew him."

"Did she ever love him, then, and had her affection changed to the cold, scornful pity, I remember ? I had rather think there had been a mistake all along."

"I had rather you were less inquisitive and less disposed to judge. People's motives for their actions are not always just so plain and straightforward that one can explain them in half-a-dozen words. I believe the actors often don't know what is in their own minds, and I am sure the bystanders ought to be very careful

not to judge hastily. I could not bear to think that
my dear friend had done such a wicked thing as to
marry without loving, yet I am afraid she was not quite
clear from a mixture of motives. I used to say there
were two Sydney St. Ermes. The Sydney who seemed
almost to belong to us at Lyllen Rectory ; who read
out-of-the-way, old-fashioned books to please my father,
and studied Hebrew with Clement in the old cedar
parlour, and drew and gardened with your mother,
and pottered about the village and the schools with me,
putting new life and delight for all of us into each
pursuit she mingled in. Then there was Lord St.
Erme's Sydney, the great minister's only daughter,
and secretary and councillor, people said; the confidante
of his schemes, the head of his household, to whose
tact and brilliancy in society he owed (so it was
believed) something of his great popularity and power.
I did not know how different the two Sydneys were
till I went to stay a few weeks in London, and saw
for myself how the sun of our little world shone in
its own sphere. I remember how dazzled I was, and
with what amazement I looked at her when she came
among us again. Mr. Edgecombe was Lord St. Erme's
nephew, and a sort of political pupil of his. He passed
for a man of considerable talent, as long as he allowed

himself to be influenced by the two St. Ermes, father and daughter. I fancy he had loved her almost from a child, and the father, foreseeing a distinguished career before him, wished them to marry."

"And she—that is what I want to know—did she wish it herself?"

"The brilliant, ambitious Sydney did. I suppose I had better tell you at once that there had been other feelings and hopes. Poor Clement was the victim among us all. It was very hard upon him; such opportunities of intimate intercourse and such a long suspense. You must not suppose there was ever any engagement; but Clement had spoken of his love to her, and had not been repulsed. Lord St. Erme did not forbid them to think of each other, he only asked for a year's delay, and during all that year I foolishly kept up Clement's hopes and my own. I knew *our* Sydney so much the best; I could not help forgetting the other. It was very injudicious, and I suffered for it, by seeing how much worse the disappointment was to Clement when it came."

"He died, did he not?"

"Five years after, of a fever in the West Indies. No, no; the disappointment had nothing to do with that. I am afraid life had lost all outward personal happiness for him, but he was too sterling a character not to know how to do without that."

"He was the best off of the two. I understand the whole story now. She gave up the man she could really have loved, for the man that she thought would win the most distinction in the world, and found she had miscalculated even for that. How bitter the waking-up must have been, to find her husband neither love-able, nor great, nor even estimable. How could she and her father be so mistaken, since they were both so wise?"

"I did not say they were *wise*. It was not exactly wisdom of which they had so much. They were just the people to overrate the talents of a pupil or lover; so overflowingly full of intelligence themselves, that they were always mistaking the reflection of their own brilliancy, for talent in their associates. Have you not noticed how apt Mrs. Edgecombe still is to fancy those she loves, cleverer than they are; and how her favourites always do show to the best advantage while she is talking with them?"

"I know I am often tempted to think myself clever when I am with her."

"And perhaps to overrate others who live in the halo of her attractiveness."

"No, no; I do not think so. But do you suppose Mrs. Edgecombe found out her mistake soon?"

"I fancy she would never have been completely un-deceived, if only her husband's devotion to her and to her father had continued. Unhappily some meddling person put it into Mr. Edgecombe's head that the world thought he was ruled by his wife and his wife's father. His pride and obstinacy took alarm, and to vindicate his independence he broke with Lord St. Erme altogether, and took office under the opposite party in politics. His deficiency of judgment, and his faults of temper, soon came out; his new colleagues could not act with him, and he had to retire into private life, a thoroughly disappointed, evil-tempered man. Sydney was deeply wounded by his desertion of her father, and utterly disapproved of all his subse-quent proceedings, though she never allowed the dis-agreements between them to appear. She yielded to all his wishes, and as you know, made herself a perfect slave to him when his health failed. Yet I am afraid even to the last, she was utterly divided from him in heart. His harshness to his son was a perpetual source of disagreement, and when Walter Edgecombe was at last driven from Combe she could not recover the blow."

"I remember how miserable it always was at Combe

while poor Mr. Edgecombe lived, but brighter days have come now. Why do you speak so very sadly?—somehow as if you thought it could possibly all come over again."

"Because I am afraid that she may again be falling into something like her old mistake. I would not have spoken of the past, if I had not thought it might help you to understand what is going on now. I am afraid her eagerness and love of rule may be misleading her again. She can't let people who live near her be themselves. She thrusts her own feelings and aims into their minds, and refuses to see anything else there. It is a sort of loving tyranny that active-minded women are prone to fall into, always at the risk of estranging from themselves utterly those people in whose lives they have usurped an undue share. Clemency, take care that she does not mislead you. Don't mistake her wishes for your own, or—or—read other people's characters and hearts with her eyes." Aunt Bessie's voice faltered over her last sentence, and when no answer came she put her hand on Clemency's averted head, and gently drew it upwards that she might look into her eyes.

She saw more trouble and consciousness there than she expected, and after one glance she sank back on her couch again, and sighed.

There was a few minutes' silence, and then Clemency, anxious to bring the conversation back to safer topics, said, "What was Uncle Clement like? Was he as beautiful as Rolla? I always fancy him like Rolla."

"You are more like what he was than Rolla, yet with a great difference."

"Very great, I am sure, the difference must be. You said just now that he was worth too much not to be able to bear to go on living after he had lost all hope of outward personal happiness. I am afraid, now, that I have not nearly so much courage. There are some sorrows that I can fancy bearing bravely and being better for, but not such a bitter sort of sorrow as loving as he had loved, and being thrown over for a less worthy person. I fancy I could bear to be rejected for a better than myself. I should see the justice of it. I should glory in the person I loved choosing nobly, even if it were not me; but to see a mere sham hero preferred, —it would be a dreadful shake to all one's ideas of justice and right. It would make everything seem unreal."

"Yes, indeed, if you had been setting up an idol so high in your heart that you could recognise no other standard of right than his or her approval. It would be an inevitable shock, however, in that case; for no

one ever does erect a fellow-creature into a god in
that fashion, without having to suffer for it sooner or
later."

"Aunt Bessie, I wish you had not said that. Now
I know what Mrs. Edgecombe means by complaining
that you chill her with sad philosophy."

"Not philosophy, my dear, experience; but I will
say no more. I did not want to send you away from
me chilled, only armed. Is not that the carriage?
What will your godmother say to me for giving
you up to her with such a grave, pale face? Is she
coming in herself?—no; that is the Colonel's voice and
step in the hall. Let me have one good look at you
before you put on your hood. Ah, that is right, no one
can find fault with your cheeks, for they are bright
enough now. I think Mrs. Edgecombe will be satisfied
with you."

CHAPTER XIII.

She was a queen of noble Nature's crowning,
A smile of hers was like an act of grace ;
She had no winsome looks, no pretty frowning
Like daily beauties of the vulgar race :
But if she smiled, a light was on her face,
A clear, cool kindliness, a lunar beam
Of peaceful radiance, silvering o'er the stream
Of human thought, with unabiding glory.
Hartley Coleridge.

MRS. EDGECOMBE was quite satisfied, though the brilliant colour that glowed on Clemency's cheeks when she entered the carriage faded soon, and left her face showing paler than usual in the setting of her black hood. To her partial eye every change in her favourite's countenance was a new beauty. Colonel Edgecombe was too busy letting down and putting up windows, and settling and resettling himself in different corners of the carriage, to have apparently much observation to bestow on any one ; yet, when they came in sight of the Red House he uttered an exclamation of dismay, and declared he had had no idea they should reach their destination so soon. He was just prepared to begin to talk himself into a proper frame of mind to encounter the coming ordeal. He did not feel ready to face the multitude yet. "Would it be wicked to order the coachman to drive two or three miles further down the road, and come very slowly back?"

"And throw Mrs. Franklyn into a nervous fever from prolonged expectation," Mrs. Edgecombe exclaimed; "to say nothing of the dog-in-the-manger selfishness of keeping Miss Franklyn in the dark to ourselves, instead of letting the rest of the world see her. I wonder you dare suggest such a thing. I am more reasonable and more magnanimous, Clemency. I don't like the people you are going among, any better than he does; but I will not cheat them of any of their pleasure. I give you up for the rest of the evening."

"But I don't," Colonel Edgecombe said, quickly, and rather low, as he was handing her from the carriage. "I want to tell you something. I have a favour to ask you. Don't let other people engross you so much, that you have no time to spare for me."

"I am not likely to be tempted," Clemency answered. "Though this is my own house, I am afraid I have not made myself useful enough in it, to be much sought after. I shall have plenty of leisure."

They were rather late, and their entrance caused some bustle. It seemed to Clemency as if every one in the room left off talking or dancing to stare at them, and whisper to each other. She was glad when Colonel Edgecombe took her from her conspicuous place by Mrs. Edgecombe's side at the upper end of the room, to join a quadrille that was forming when they entered.

Clemency's experience of dancing was small, and she had to give her mind to the figure as long as she was called upon to take part in it ; but when the next set were dancing she was ready to talk and look about and enjoy herself.

" Oh, look ! " she exclaimed, to Colonel Edgecombe. " How pretty ! Is not that a pretty sight ? "

" Where ! What ? "

" There ! The reflection in that glass, from the other end of the room, of Sydney Serle dancing. She is crossing the figure again. Now, look ! In a white dress with a white wreath on her head. How prettily she moves and turns her head to speak to her partner. I hope your mother will be just enough to admire her to-night. I never saw her so lovely and bright before. It is quite a picture."

" My mother will only have eyes for one person to-night. But who in the world is that ponderous, heavy fellow, cutting ridiculous capers before Miss Serle just now, and looking so solemnly self-satisfied all the time ? "

" That is Mr. Humphreys, a medical man, from Hemsley. I hardly know him ; but I persuaded Mrs. Franklyn to ask him to-night because I heard a rumour that he was engaged to Sydney Serle, and I thought she would like him to be here. I wonder whether it is true ? "

" True ! How absurd ! It can't possibly be true. Just look at them—Beauty and the Beast ! "

" Come, that is rather hard on Mr. Humphreys. He may be a very worthy man, though he does dance oddly. As for looks—hem !—I don't see, for my part, that he is much uglier than other people."

" Perhaps not. You are right. I understand what you mean : there is another edition of Beauty and the Beast reflected in the glass beyond us. I caught a glimpse of it as we passed just now, and quite acknowledge the resemblance."

" That shows how much you are always thinking of yourself. I did not look in the glass ; and I was not thinking of you at all. I only meant that Mr. Humphreys is not uglier than a man has a right to be. If people can be beautiful it is very well, and one is much obliged to them ; but it is not what one expects of men. I have seen one beautiful man—but that is all."

"Who can you mean? Have I seen him?"

"Oh, yes; very often."

"Do you mean Arthur Yonge? I suppose he is handsome, but——"

"Oh dear no. I meant old Mr. Serle. Surely you have noticed how beautiful he is, with his soft white hair and radiantly benevolent face, especially when he is pointing out some pretty prospect in Combe valley, or speaking to his daughter. She looks very like him to-night."

Colonel Edgecombe had been hoping all day to find an opportunity of privately asking Clemency to take the Serles under her special protection, and shield them from any neglect to which their strangeness to the Red-House society might expose them. This was the favour he had spoken about; but now, when the best possible opening for asking it presented itself, he hesitated. Dancing began again before he had made up his mind; and as he and Clemency went through the last figure of the quadrille almost in silence, he decided that he would not say anything to her about the Serles. He discovered that he should be very sorry for Clemency to misunderstand him, and he was convinced that if she supposed him more interested in them than a good neighbour might be, it would be a misunderstanding. The sight of Sydney's pretty face turned smilingly and .

brightly towards her uncouth partner, had not struck
him as pleasantly as it had struck Clemency. If Miss
Serle could be made happy so easily, there was
surely no occasion for him to quarrel with his mother
for the sake of championing her. He need feel no
responsibility on her account if she were one of those
girls who could be pleased by any one's notice, and
who dreaded nothing but being left alone. This
conviction kept him lingering at Clemency's side,
long after the dance was ended; for the greater
part of the evening, in fact. Clemency did not soon
dance again; there was a scarcity of gentlemen, and as
she felt responsible for the enjoyment of the young
lady guests, she refused to take up a place, and devoted
herself to finding partners for some, and consoling
others who were necessarily left out. Colonel Edgecombe placed himself under her orders to be made
useful in any way she pleased; but he contrived to cut
the waltzes and polkas, for which he was victimised, so
short, that he soon ceased to be a favourite partner.

Whenever Clemency paused from her task of making
conversation, or looked round for a messenger to bring
an old lady her shawl, or to hunt up some forgotten
damsel's tardy partner, she was sure to find him near
her, ready and waiting to do her pleasure. With

such an efficient helper the duties of the evening were pleasant and easy enough. She had thanks and compliments paid her on her unselfish conduct in seeking every one's gratification rather than her own, and she felt ashamed of listening to them. She knew she was not giving up anything, and that the gay temper every one was praising, was easy enough to preserve with such a dancing heart as she had.

Meanwhile, without any need of Colonel Edgecombe's countenance, Sydney was filling the unexpected position of belle of the ball. Other young ladies had to wait patiently for partners, and take their turn in sitting still, but she was constantly surrounded by a little circle of admirers, and had so many applications for every dance that she grew weary of refusing. Mr. Humphreys had been wise in securing her for several dances before she knew how popular she was destined to be; but no one else had a chance of being so distinguished. He became quite an object of envy to several people; and his tall, talkative sisters, of whom Sydney stood so much in awe, took a little credit to themselves for being more intimate with her, than any other person in the room could claim to be. She was "our dear Sydney," "our sweet, charming Sydney," whenever they spoke of her, and they contrived to hedge her round with their attention and care, so as to make it difficult for any one to get near her except their own friends. The part of the room occupied by the Misses Humphreys and their special clique was, through the evening, the centre of all the merriment and noisy talk that went on.

As Colonel Edgecombe passed and repassed the group, in performing Clemency's errands, he now and then detected amidst the hubbub of voices, a little shrill, affected laugh, which sounded like a most unpleasant mockery and exaggeration of the sounds he had thought so sweet in the Manor Combe sitting-room. Once or twice he caught Sydney's eye as he passed her in dancing, but he tried not to see the wistful, appealing glance there. He had made up his mind to believe that she was enjoying herself thoroughly among her friends ; and the idea of disputing her company with such people as the Humphreys was very distasteful to him. If she were content and well amused, that was enough, he said many times to himself, without, however, being the least able to dispel an unaccountable sense of annoyance and dissatisfaction that hung over him. Why had he put off his journey for this wearisome evening, when his presence could so well have been dispensed with ? He promised himself that he would never again be deluded into making sacrifices by believing himself important even to such modest seeming people as old Mr. Serle and Sydney. Towards the close of the evening he danced again with Clemency; the bright simplicity of her manner was a rest to him in his present irritable mood.

"I know how it is that you and my mother get on so well together," he said, as they were walking round the room after the dance was over. "You are the right person for restless natures like hers and mine to be near. You are not always thinking of yourself as we are, so you are not open to the thousand pin-point wounds, we self-occupied ones bring upon ourselves."

"Your mother looks very happy to-night; it is a great triumph to have brought her through a whole evening at the Red House, without one pin-point wound. If you have got her share you must not mind. It was impossible for every one to escape, for I have told you often, have I not, that the atmosphere of the Red House is full of little arrows of annoyance. They must fall on some one. I am sorry, that just to-night, it should have been you."

It was more than a pin-point wound to Clemency to observe the cloud that had come over her companion's brow; but she had not courage to ask its cause. They

were just passing a bench where the Misses Humphreys
and Sydney were seated ; several gentlemen stood
before them, and the talking and laughter sounded a
little uproarious.

"The atmosphere of the Red House seems to be
wonderfully exhilarating to some people at all events,"
Colonel Edgecombe remarked, with an accent of intense
annoyance, that made Clemency think he outdid his
mother in fastidiousness.

"You surely don't object to the Misses Humphreys
amusing themselves in their own way?" she said.

"Certainly not. It is good to see it. Excitement
shows people's characters as they really are : one gets a
glimpse of what *is their own way,* as you observe. In
a mixed company like this each one seeks his proper
element."

"That is a very unfair remark, if you are thinking of
Sydney Serle," cried Clemency, moved to speak by her
quick sense of justice. "She can't help those noisy,
forward people monopolising her, for we have left her to
them all the evening. I am sure she does not really
prefer them. I observed her just now when we passed
her in the dance, and her face was so wistful and depressed, when she was not speaking, that my conscience
smote me. Flushed cheeks and quick talking don't prove

happiness in Sydney Serle. They are far more often tokens, that she is so frightened she does not know what she is saying. Her real happy look is very different. I have studied her, because your mother misunderstands her sometimes a little, you know, and I have to explain —to stand up for her."

" I perceive that you can't bear to hear any one blamed."

" Oh, yes, I can. Fastidious people, for example, who won't let their neighbours laugh as loud as they please. You will never hear me say a word in their favour."

" I shall not hear it; but behind my back you will make excuses for me too. Peace-making is your vocation, as I have experienced over and over again. You make everything clear. Does Miss Serle know what a generous champion she has in you, with my mother ?"

" I should not like her to know she wants a champion. She values your mother's good opinion above everything else in the world, and naturally a little grudges me the lion's share. Your mother is unjust, you know, in her division of favour between her goddaughters; and feeling that, I am rather shy of forcing myself on Sydney. Yet I wish I had been more attentive to her to-night; I have made one attempt to deliver her from the Humphreys' set, but I think now I ought

to have been more persevering. Have you courage
to make a descent upon them and bear Sydney off to
your mother and me? Poor old Mr. Serle was looking
so forlorn an hour ago, that I took him into the tea-
room, where I believe he is fast asleep among the
shawls and opera cloaks. Sydney may be wondering
where he is; will you go and tell her?"

"If you send me away and order me to go, I will."

"Yes, certainly; I think it ought to be done."

He walked once more down the room with her;
there was a hesitation in his manner, and a reluctance
to leave her, which she could not help perceiving.

When he had restored her to her seat by Mrs. Edgecombe, he said, "So I am to go and bring Miss Serle
here. You really think I ought. You are sure she
wishes to get away from those people?"

"Quite sure. What a coward you are; go."

Sydney had been feeling all the evening as if she
had been moving about in a dream,—in one of her own
day-dreams, realised to the letter. A great part of her
life was spent in enacting fictitious scenes; and as her
imagination had an extremely limited range—her
brightest and her most doleful visions rarely figuring
any higher joys or deeper pangs than those of supremely
gratified or cruelly mortified vanity—her dreams had a

better chance than most people's of being literally fulfilled. The strangeness of the evening was that the
two extremes, the brightest vision and the darkest, met
together, and were fulfilled at the same moment, with
the cruel mockery of each other that belongs to dreams.
For the first hour or so, before the Edgecombes came,
and for a little time afterwards, she was supremely
happy. The lights, the music, the quick movements,
the brightly-dressed company, the admiring looks and
whispered words of praise that followed her about, were
all very wonderful and new to her. It was like getting
into fairy-land, into the sort of tinsel fairy-land, at
least, which her fancy was accustomed to call up. She
was only afraid of waking suddenly and finding herself sewing in the Manor Combe sitting-room.

It disturbed her a little to have to fill up her card of
dances so very far down. She manœuvred to leave a
few vacant places, and thought, with a sort of pleased
dismay, how strange it would be to be obliged to tell
Colonel Edgecombe when he came and stood before her,
so very tall and imposing as he would look, that she
could only give him such and such a dance. Would he
be very much surprised ? She went on figuring that
little scene to herself in time to the music for several
dances, even after the High-Combe party had entered

the ball-room, but when the quadrille she had destined for him came, and she had to take one of her previously rejected partners, her spirits began to flag, and the wistful look Clemency had noticed, replaced the happy smiles on her face.

As she walked down the room, after the quadrille was over, she met Mrs. Edgecombe, who paid her a little compliment on her dress, and stroked her cheek with one finger of her gloved hand, precisely with that manner of indulgent elder to a pretty spoilt child, which of all her manners had the most extinguishing effect on poor Sydney. Mr. and the Misses Humphreys came up at this unpropitious moment, and Mrs. Edgecombe begged to be introduced to Sydney's kind friends, and told her before them all, that since she knew so few people in the room, she was fortunate in having such a careful *chaperone* as Mrs. Humphreys seemed to be. She advised her not to allow herself to be separated from her friends, as she could not expect her father to take much trouble in looking after her, and she ought not to go about alone.

The Humphreys' party seemed to multiply and enlarge before Sydney's eyes, as Mrs. Edgecombe spoke, till the whole room seemed to be full of faces beaming with exultation as theirs beamed, and mocking her. After that, though she struggled hard to keep up the appearance of enjoyment, she felt as people feel when a delightful dream gradually changes into an oppressive nightmare. Yet it was rather bewilderment than pain she suffered. She was too busy trying to talk and laugh, and keep her lips smiling, to know exactly what was the matter. Only she had a painful sense of having lived through the scene before, and of knowing what was coming. It was her vision on the snowy day realised fully at last : the Edgecombes and Clemency—happy together in her sight, and shutting her out of their company—delivering her over to the Humphreys, who stood round her triumphant, and would not let her have freedom even to think of anything but themselves. How the incessant repetition of her name by the sisters fretted her, and how intolerable it was to know that she could not glance round the room without catching the brother's jealous eye watching the direction of hers.

Her numerous dancing engagements appeared a stratagem of the Humphreys' to divide her from the friends she wanted to join. She observed how little Colonel Edgecombe danced, and it irritated her dreadfully to think every time she stood up that she was losing a chance of receiving the one or two kind words which she fancied would make her happy again. She thought she only wanted to be assured she had not done anything to offend him irrevocably. Her efforts at mirth grew almost desperate at last, and even unsuspicious Mr. Humphreys began to think that her laugh sounded harsh, and that her cheeks were unnaturally flushed. She was getting a little over-excited, he did not scruple to tell her, and he really must insist—yes, insist, on her giving up the last polka, and resting for a time. The air of the room was oppressive, he observed, and though he was well aware of the danger of sudden changes of temperature, yet he thought that well wrapped up in his mother's shawl, and with him to select the least draughty walks, Miss Serle might be benefited by a short walk in the garden. He should not hesitate to sanction such a course, imprudent as some might deem it, by taking Miss Serle into the open air himself.

Sydney was combating this proposition with a vehemence which showed how little hope she had of carrying her point, when Colonel Edgecombe came up with Clemency's message. He stood so upright before her, spoke so distinctly, and offered his arm with such a grave determined air, that even the Misses Humphreys had not presence of mind to make an objection. Sydney gave one little frightened glance up into his face, and then rose and placed her hand on his arm without a word. She had not been used to see his face without a smile upon it lately, or to be spoken to in that formal tone, and it made her heart sink. She felt like a frightened child going to be scolded. What had she done? She knew she had been talking a little fast and a little loud; was Mrs. Edgecombe very much displeased, and would she tell her so before him? The idea grew too dreadful to be borne, and when they were quite out of hearing of the Humphreys, she found courage to remonstrate.

"I am so tired, and the room is so crowded, I had rather not walk up to the top again. Did you not say that papa was in the tea-room? May I go to him instead of to Mrs. Edgecombe? I dare say he is wanting me, and will be glad to go home."

"Certainly; my mother and Miss Franklyn will be leaving immediately, and I am sure they would not like you to go to them if you are tired. What a crush there is round the door! Let us walk through the conservatory out into the garden, we can get to the tea-room that way."

A fresh dance was beginning; they met a stream of people coming in from the garden, and had to proceed slowly. Once they were crushed up against a bench, on which sat two or three ladies, of whose conversation they could not avoid hearing a sentence or two.

"Mrs. Edgecombe did not contradict when I congratulated her. I assure you, there can be no doubt that it is an engagement. I have it on the best authority."

"Well, I am glad to hear it," the other answered. "Miss Franklyn is a great favourite of mine, and I think Colonel Edgecombe has made a wise choice."

Colonel Edgecombe pushed on impatiently when the names reached his ears, and in a minute more they were free of the crowd, and in the now deserted conservatory. It was shabbily filled with flowers, but gleaming with coloured lamps; and when Colonel Edgecombe glanced at Sydney, to see if she were embarrassed at what they had overheard, he hoped it might be the effect of the lights that made her cheeks look so ghastly pale. He made a trifling remark, and she did not answer; then he felt that her hand trembled on his arm, and saw that she was shivering as if with cold.

"You ought not to have come here, you have no shawl on; let me take you back to my mother and Miss Franklyn."

"Oh, no, not to them. I can't go to them," Sydney said, quickly.

The words came out almost against her will, and she was as much startled as Colonel Edgecombe at the wail of pain in which they were uttered. She hardly knew the voice; it was not like herself speaking. The fresh air of the garden revived her, she made a great effort to control the trembling of her limbs, and to quicken her pace.

"I had rather go at once to papa, please," she said, in her natural voice. "I think I am over-tired."

No other word was spoken while they walked down the gravel-walk in front of the house; but when they approached an open glass-door at the further end, Colonel Edgecombe suddenly placed his hand on the still trembling fingers on his arm, and said, "I must ask you a question. Did you hear what that old woman said just now?"

"Yes, I did," Sydney answered, her voice shaking terribly.

"Well, it was not true, it was utterly untrue, every word."

"Oh!" was all Sydney could say. It sounded very much as if she rolled a weight off her heart in breathing the word; and yet she went on walking quickly and did not raise her eyes.

"One minute more," Colonel Edgecombe said, drawing her back. "Sydney, are you glad that it is not true? do you care about it?"

"Yes," Sydney faltered, and then she did look up and saw two dark, searching eyes anxiously reading her face. They softened wonderfully as they met hers.

"Thank you, dear Sydney, for being so true," he answered. He took her other hand in his, and they stood for a breathless minute silently looking at each other, and then the sound of voices floating through the open door seemed to divide them.

Sydney snatched away her hand and entered the room, now crowded with cloaked and shawled ladies, waiting for their carriages. Colonel Edgecombe did not follow her, she stood still till the sound of his footsteps crushing the gravel died away along the walk, and then she came forward into the light.

Old Mr. Serle, just disturbed from a comfortable nap on the sofa, was too much bewildered by the bustle to which he had awakened, to notice anything unusual in his daughter's manner. He was glad to find Sydney as eager to return home as he was, and did not trouble her with any questions about her enjoyment of the evening.

He expatiated on the lateness, or rather earliness, of

the hour, and upon Lizzie's probable remarks about the strangeness of their coming in to go to bed just as other people were beginning their day's work—all through the drive—while Sydney looked out of the carriage-window persistently, and yet saw nothing of the summer sunrise, which dawned, and deepened, and glowed above the Combe woods, and flooded the little valley from end to end with light, before they reached the Manor.

CHAPTER XIV.

O brich den Faden nicht der Freundshaft rasch entzwei,
Wird er auch neu geknüft, ein knoten bleibt dabei.

Rückert.

COLONEL EDGECOMBE left Combe the morning after
the ball, and Mrs. Edgecombe found the loneliness of
the house so oppressive after his departure, that she
never rested till she had brought Miss Arnays and
Clemency from Tunstall, to spend the time of his
absence with her. Miss Arnays had suffered a good
deal from the heat, and had felt the closeness of the
town very much ever since the summer weather set in
this year, and her niece and her old friend both flattered
themselves that the change to country air would restore
her health, which had been failing gradually during the
last few months. They did not confess their fears for
her even to each other, for they could neither of them
bear yet to put them into words; but the unspoken
anxiety they shared drew them closer together than

they had ever been before. Clemency felt sometimes as if she were taking her aunt's place in Mrs. Edgecombe's full confidence. She had been treated like a spoilt child in that house hitherto—allowed to take liberties and encouraged to speak her mind with a freedom no one else ventured on ; now Mrs. Edgecombe seemed disposed to trust her and consult her like a full-grown daughter or an equal friend.

It was a grave but very happy visit. Miss Arnays seemed to have brought her own still peace into the great house ; the heavy gloom and stateliness of former days was quite gone, and the excitement that Colonel Edgecombe had introduced had subsided for the time.

Every now and then, long letters came from Colonel Edgecombe, which his mother, after hastily glancing through, generally passed on as a matter of course to Clemency, to be read aloud. " He does not write such a quantity just for me, you may be sure, my dear," she said once, in answer to Clemency's scruples, thus effectually putting a stop to further remonstrance. They were pleasant, easy letters to read aloud. Colonel Edgecombe, after spending a few days in London, had accompanied the old Indian friend, whom he had gone to London to meet, on a tour in the Highlands, and his histories of the adventures they shared, and the acquaintances they fell in with, were very clever and entertaining. They were written at the expense of some time and labour, with an evident desire to give his mother pleasure; but the letters were such as any stranger might read all through, there were none of the intimate allusions to past events, or to very private thoughts and feelings in them, which had made Mrs. Edgecombe jealous of ever letting her son's Indian letters pass out of her own hands. Miss Franklyn's name came in now and then: when Clemency saw it on the page, she had a little difficulty in reading on steadily; but it always turned out to be quite a casual mention. He had thought how Miss Franklyn would like to sketch such a scene; or his friend had done or said something of which Miss Franklyn would have approved; or he had met a young lady at one of the houses where he was visiting, who was something in Miss Franklyn's style, though not nearly so handsome.

There was often a postscript, or extra page to the letter, filled with answers to questions on matters of business his mother had asked, or with directions respecting some of the works on the estate, in which he had just begun to take an interest when he went away. Mrs. Edgecombe usually put these aside at the first reading of the letters; but before the day was over Clemency was sure to be called to a private consultation over their contents, and she soon began to take a greater interest in them than in any other part of the letters. She found herself recalling sentences sometimes with a vague apprehension that she saw another meaning in them than did the person to whom they were addressed.

Mrs. Edgecombe, during the last years of her husband's life, while he was incapacitated by illness, and since his death, had taken a very active part in the management of the Edgecombe property. She had a real genius for government, and she had laboured with great energy and success to restore order and prosperity to the estate, which had been impaired by Mr. Edgecombe's long mismanagement. When her son returned to England, she had attempted to resign everything into his hands; but partly through indolence and partly through unwillingness to thrust her aside, he had been very slow in assuming the authority that properly belonged to him. Just now the little jars that will occur, in ever so small a kingdom, whenever there are two acknowledged rulers with undefined powers, were beginning to be felt. As Clemency read and pondered over rather incoherent sentences in Colonel Edgecombe's letters, in which (while disclaiming all intention of interfering with any of his mother's arrangements) he stated wishes diametrically opposed to hers, she felt as if she were watching the little cloud rising which might hereafter overshadow all her friend's sky. Mrs. Edgecombe dwelt upon the earnest entreaties that she would consult her own pleasure about everything, which really made up the largest part of every message, but Clemency could not help noticing the quiet masculine assumption of being necessarily in the right, which peeped out through all the show of acquiescence and deference. She did not like the writer any less for showing that he understood his rightful place in the household, and would hereafter inevitably take it; and her thoughts were kept busy about him and his doings, by the insight she thus acquired into the difficulties of his position, and the necessity for unusual generosity and forbearance, which his mother's peculiar character and exacting affection laid upon him. She hoped, with almost an agony of hoping, that he would prove equal to the task laid upon him, and she allowed her fancy full scope to picture out beautiful ways of acting, and generous sacrifices which should make his life a model of filial duty.

Mrs. Edgecombe counted confidently on having her time, and thoughts, and sympathy, always at her service; and whenever she or Clemency were alone together, the differences of opinion between herself and her son, referred to in the letters, were discussed endlessly. Clemency had a happy hour whenever she thought she had succeeded in making any part of Colonel Edgecombe's meaning clearer than it had been before without giving his mother pain, or when she had managed to have a more conciliating word inserted in the reply, than had been at first proposed. It was wonderful how closely this confidence knit the two together, and how the difference of age and position seemed to vanish before the common reading of each other's hearts, which accord in one purpose brought about.

Clemency's affection for her godmother seemed to take the character of an absorbing passion in those days; she fancied that her whole life could be well given up to the task of standing between her oversensitive nature and possible pain. She hardly knew how much the thought of saving some one else from the wrong of inflicting the pain, mixed with her anxiety; or that it was the pictured ideally beautiful life she was longing to guard, as well as the broken-down suffering one, she actually saw before her. The extreme disappointment she felt when a sentence in one of Colonel Edgecombe's letters was less considerate than she had expected beforehand that it would be, was the penalty she paid for dreaming. And after a time, when a question remotely concerning Mr. Serle's interest came into the discussion, she not unfrequently had the disappointment to bear.

As she sat in the garden one hot summer afternoon, pondering over the angry words of a letter received from Colonel Edgecombe that morning, which Mrs. Edgecombe had begged her to re-read, and recalling the deep flush of pain that had suffused her friend's face on first hearing it, and the weight of aching anxiety that had hung on her brow since, she felt less hopeful about the future peace of Combe than she had ever been before. The glorious afternoon light glowed on the dark red walls and picturesque stone carvings of the old house; but it did not look bright in Clemency's eyes. The cloud of care and apprehension which, to her fancy, had belonged to Combe since she knew it, was hanging over it still, and she began to think now it would always be there. The conviction did not by any means lessen her affection for the place; the prospect of sharing trouble with those she loved was the closest and dearest bond of all to her. She had never before felt her life so bound up with the Combe life, or been so content as she was just then, to let her own image mix with her visions of the future that was to be enacted there.

A sort of joyful courage came in the place of fear, as she went on musing; and when the time arrived for her to return to the house, she was surprised to find that she had let the whole afternoon slip away without coming to any conclusion on the question Mrs. Edgecombe had asked her to ponder over; also, that she was in brighter spirits than she could give any satisfactory reason for.

She stood at the bottom of the door-steps for a minute or two to reflect soberly on what was really going on within the house, lest she should bring discordantly bright smiles into the gloom pervading it. Mrs. Edgecombe met her in the hall, both hands stretched out, and such a face of beaming delight as Clemency had only seen once before.

" The letter, Clemency!" she said; "give me the letter to tear up, and never think of again. There!" she said, tearing it into a hundred pieces, and scattering them into the garden; " it has gone, gone, gone! Oh, what a relief! Now guess why I am so happy."

"You have heard again."

"Better, far. He is here—Walter—he has been with me more than an hour. Oh, Clemency! he has such a good kind heart! and he knows so well what a foolish woman his mother is. He had not a moment's peace after he had despatched that letter till he was on his way home to see how I had taken it. He wrote in a hurry, on the impulse of a moment, he says, and it did not occur to him till afterwards, that I might be hurt by his words; that I might think he meant to blame me. It was not quite *that* I thought. I did him a greater injustice still. The first look on his face set him right with me; I wanted no words. Oh, how happy I am!"

"I am glad you are happy; I am glad he has come," Clemency said, hastily; but as they were crossing the hall, she added in rather a more doubtful tone, "Has he changed his mind, then? Has he given up to you about the Serles?"

"The Serles? We have not mentioned them. The only conclusion we have come to is, that we are never to write to each other about business again, and then there can never be another misunderstanding. We shall only have one way when we are together. The Serles—my dear, the Serles might have the whole estate, if only they

did not come between my son and me. Is it possible
you could think it was the money I cared about?"

There was not time for Clemency to say that she had
been as much puzzled by the quarrel as she now was by
the hasty reconciliation; they had reached the library,
and Mrs. Edgecombe paused with her hand on the door
to say,—

"You must forgive me, Clemency, that I could not
help letting Walter know the share you have had in
our discussions. He says that your suggestions are the
only wise ones that have been made in the whole
business, and he is excessively obliged to you. Don't
be surprised if he talks to you as if you knew all."

Clemency's first thought after entering the library
was that Mrs. Edgecombe's last sentence might have
been spared. To judge by Colonel Edgecombe's embarrassed manner of coming to meet her, and the deep
flush that came into his face as they shook hands, there
was very little danger of his being too communicative.
It was quite a new thing to see him shy and ill at ease,
and Clemency could only conclude that explanations
were less to his taste than to his mother's, and that the
last hour's interview had cost something to his English
reserve and horror of everything like a scene. She
fancied even that for some reason Mrs. Edgecombe's

extreme gaiety jarred upon him, and that when once or twice his eye rested on her radiant face, his own grew clouded. After the first moment of meeting was over, however, he was extremely cordial and friendly in his manner to her; and when she left the library to go to her aunt's room, he followed her into the hall to say for the twentieth time,—

"I am particularly glad you are here. You can't think what a relief it was to me to find you and your aunt still with my mother. You, who have so much more influence with her than anyone else."

Miss Arnays was not able to join the rest of the party at dinner that day ; and Clemency having begged Mrs. Edgecombe not to wait for her, lingered in her aunt's room, making tea for her, and reading her to sleep afterwards ; so that when she entered the dining-room, dinner was half over, and Mrs. Edgecombe seemed already to have tired herself with talking to a dull companion.

"You must think of something to tell us," she said, as soon as Clemency was seated. "Walter has been cross-questioning me about the whole neighbourhood, and I have told him every scrap of gossip I can recollect or invent. Yet he complains that I know nothing about anyone. He says we must have turned High

Combe into a nunnery, and lived in seclusion since he left."

" Weaving all manner of webs out of your brains like spiders, mother," Colonel Edgecombe said, " and letting the whole world outside go its way without heeding. I don't suppose you have so much as looked into a newspaper since I left. There might have been several revolutions in Europe, and two or three wars might have broken out, without your knowing anything about it."

" Mrs. Edgecombe read the newspapers eagerly enough while one war was going on," cried Clemency.

" That is just what I complain of," he said, " the exclusive importance you (I am speaking of women in general) give to your own concerns. Why should newspapers be only worth reading when you expect to see a name you know in them. If you took more general interest in public affairs you would be much happier."

" Very true ; only it is a truism that does not particularly concern your mother and me. You are very inconsistent in your fault-finding. Don't you remember, when we were busy arranging those Indian antiquities the last time I was staying here, how you used to grumble at us for going to the world before the flood for interests, instead of confining ourselves to the flower-garden."

"The Indian antiquities degenerated into furniture belonging to your world the house, as soon as you began to arrange them in cabinets; but come, I will be candid, and confess that I am inconsistent; I really had quite forgotten that old grievance. There must be something essentially soothing in fault-finding, since even I fly to it for consolation after a dusty journey."

"I am glad you are in a candid frame of mind, for now I can say something I was beginning to think I must suppress, till you had left the room, for fear of your triumphing over us. I heard a piece of news just before I came downstairs to dinner, which made me think we *had* been shutting ourselves up from our neighbours too long. Do you know," turning to Mrs. Edgecombe, "that poor Sydney Serle has been very unwell ever since the night of the ball at the Red House? I missed her from her place at church on Sunday, but I supposed she was from home. I wish I had asked. Did you know she was ill?"

"Not I! It is her own fault for not telling me. She can't be too ill to send a message or write a note, and I would have gone to her directly. I do so dislike people to make martyrs of themselves in that provoking sort of way, as if one must know by intuition when there is anything amiss with them. I dare say the foolish child is fretting about not seeing me, and yet forbidding everyone in the house to let me know she is ill."

"Who told you Miss Serle was ill ? what have you heard ? " Colonel Edgecombe asked, sharply, as if to interrupt his mother's tirade.

"Mr. Humphreys told Aunt Bessie this afternoon. He came to see her while I was out ; and finding her alone, he (as everyone else does) unburdened his mind to her of his anxiety about Sydney Serle. He is attending her ; and he acknowledged, very unprofessionally, that he did not understand her complaint, and felt quite powerless to do her any good. At first he hoped it was only a feverish cold caught at the ball, but now he begins to be alarmed, he says she seems unable to make any effort to get well. Aunt Bessie tells me his eyes filled with tears as he spoke about his patient. He has won her heart for ever by showing so much feeling."

"He always looks on the worst side," Mrs. Edgecombe put in. "I am glad it is only Mr. Humphreys' opinion. You know how he has been frightening us about your aunt, Clemency ; and certainly without cause. Poor little Sydney ! I will go and see her to-morrow, and find out what can be done. If she wants change of air, we might arrange for her to go to the sea with you and your aunt, when you go. I dare say there is not much amiss. Sydney is just the person to mope unreasonably if she feels unwell."

"But I don't think anyone can be called unreasonable for moping, who is shut up in the same house with Mrs. George Serle. Fancy the torture of her step and voice in a sick-room ; besides, I can't help suspecting another reason for Sydney's depression."

There was a pause after this remark. Mrs. Edgecombe remained silent, as if she thought the subject exhausted, and Colonel Edgecombe appeared wholly occupied with a bunch of grapes he was carefully dividing with the grape scissors. But as he passed the fruit to Clemency, he said, rather low,—

"Pray go on with what you were saying. Some remark about Miss Serle, I think. You did not finish it.

"Perhaps I had better not finish it. It is only a suspicion, founded partly on my dislike of Mrs. George and partly on my observations that night of the ball."

"You can't think worse of Mrs. George than I do."

"Well, then, I think her capable of trying to marry

Sydney to Mr. Humphreys against her will. Mrs. George always speaks of Sydney as if she were a burden in the house, and I can fancy her taking almost any means to get her out of it. I can,—in spite of that unbelieving shrug of your shoulders, dear Mrs. Edgecombe. You dislike Mrs. George Serle as much as I do—how is it you do not pity Sydney more?"

"I have unfortunately too strong a belief in Sydney's willingness to marry anyone who would take her away from Combe, and endow her with the importance of being married, to pity her for any such cause as you suggest. If Mr. Humphreys wants her, he must ask her before anyone else does, that is all. She will be quite as happy with him as with anyone else. I am really very fond of poor little Sydney, but you can't make her look like a heroine to me. Stay, Walter! don't cut another bunch of grapes to pieces. We have no others ripe just now; and I think I shall send these to-night to Sydney, with a note explaining that I have only just heard of her illness, and will come and see her to-morrow. Will you look for a pretty basket in the drawing-room, Clemency, and put these grapes and some flowers in it, while I write my note? Sydney will be pleased with the attention—it will do her good.

Mrs. Edgecombe went to a side-table to write her note, and Colonel Edgecombe followed Clemency through the folding-doors into the drawing-room. As soon as they were out of hearing, he exclaimed, angrily—

"What a thing it is to live all one's life shut up in a great house! How, it spoils the best hearted people. I believe my mother thinks that any one of her Combe neighbours would be cured of the plague by a bunch of grapes, and a civil message from her. It is intolerable presumption."

"Your mother's note will be a great deal kinder than her words," Clemency ventured to say.

"But what right has she to write kind notes to Miss Serle, while she thinks and speaks of her as she has been doing just now? Does she consider sham kindness good enough for those she chooses to call inferiors? To my mind, that is the last point of insolence."

Clemency looked up surprised; and seeing a depth of annoyance in her companion's face, which clearly did not admit of being reasoned away, she turned to the window, and occupied herself silently in gathering a handful of the shining dark leaves, and a magnificent half-opened white flower of the magnolia, that grew outside. When she had got what she wanted, she took a small basket from the table, and began slowly to arrange the leaves and fruit in it, and to dispose the flower-cup in the best place on the top of her purple and green pyramid.

"I will go back to Mrs. Edgecombe for the note," she said at last. "This is, at all events, a pretty-looking peace-offering, and I am sure Sydney will put a kinder construction on its being sent than you seem disposed to do. She and I know how really kind and good our godmother has been to us all our lives. She will not suspect her of intentional neglect, you may be sure."

Colonel Edgecombe preceded Clemency to the door and half opened it ; but instead of letting her pass, he turned round, stood straight before her, barring her exit, and began to speak, hurriedly.

"What must you think of me, Miss Franklyn ?" he said. "I came here to-day, as I know you know, to atone for one outbreak of ill-humour, and ever since you have seen me I have been giving way to a worse temper than the first,—before you, too, whose good opinion I value more than any one's in the world. Can you, who make excuses for everybody, invent some for me ?"

"They will not be wanted," Clemency said. "Your

mother is so happy to have you at home again, every-thing will go well now."

"I wish I could hope it. You are the only person who understands us both—the only one who could reconcile my mother to me. If I could speak to you alone—explain myself—may I have an opportunity of speaking to you alone to-morrow, and telling you what has been long in my mind?"

"My dear Walter, let me pass—why do you block up the doorway?" Mrs. Edgecombe said, in a distinct voice, from behind.

She had come up to the folding-doors unheard by them; the last sentence had reached her ears; and finding she could neither close the doors nor retreat without attracting observation, she thought it best to make them aware of her presence at once. They started aside quickly, and she went on talking as fast as she could to spare their confusion.

"How beautifully you have arranged the basket Clemency! Here is my note to put in somewhere. Must you go upstairs again so soon? Well, if your aunt wants you, I will not keep you from her. She has had rather a lonely day—it is quite fair she should have you for the rest of the evening. Go, my dear."

When Clemency had made her escape from the

room, Mrs. Edgecombe turned eagerly to look for her son ; hoping for a happy word of explanation from him, when they were left alone together. Her heart beat very high : she thought the happy moment she had long foreseen had come at last. The room behind her was empty, however ; he had walked away while she was speaking ; and though she pursued her search into the library and even peered into the twilight of the conservatory, and called his name, she received no answer, and was obliged to conclude that he had retreated through the open window into the garden, and that he did not mean to relieve her anxiety just then.

Well, it was only waiting a few hours at the worst. The words she had heard had set her mind at rest, and she allowed herself to be very happy. She rang the bell for lights, and sat the rest of the evening in the library, listening intently for her son's step on the walk outside. She had so long imagined the delight of his coming to confide his love for Clemency to her, that she could not put herself out of the way of hearing, if he should choose to consult her that night. She waited till long after her usual hour of going upstairs. At last, very late, she heard him enter the house, walk straight upstairs, and shut himself into his room. It

was a deep disappointment to her that he should shun
her just in the crisis of his life, and something of a
surprise, too, for he surely must know how earnestly she
should sympathise and wish him success in his purpose.
Perhaps he did not like to speak of hopes that might still
seem to him very uncertain.   Since he would not come
to her for comfort, she did not pity him for the suspense he was enduring.   She was only glad she did not
share it, and could go to bed saying, confidently, to
herself, that to-morrow would be the happiest day of
her life.

Clemency, too, was late in going to bed.   It surprised and rather disconcerted her that Mrs. Edgecombe did not come as usual to spend an hour in Miss
Arnays' room during the evening.   After Miss Arnays
was in bed, Clemency sat for a long time looking
down into the moonlit garden and listening to the far-
off echoing sounds in the great quiet house.   She was
in no hurry for the morrow to come ; she had an undefined fear she could not account for, of what it might
bring.   She wished the moon could go on shining stilly
into the garden for ever, and the house rest in the
peace which to her fancy brooded over it now that the
reconciled mother and son were together there.   Friendly
words and grateful looks had made a sort of dim rest

and content in her own heart, too ; it might be very cowardly, but she rather shrank from a full glare of daylight coming in to drive them away, even with bright, clear happiness.

END OF VOL. I.

www.ingramcontent.com/pod-product-compliance
Lightning Source LLC
Chambersburg PA
CBHW021034030726
47496CB00006B/1525